ALSO BY DANIEL FUCHS

WEST OF
THE ROCKIES

WEST OF THE ROCKIES

Daniel Fuchs

Alfred A. Knopf   New York

1971

WEST OF
THE ROCKIES

BURT CLARIS WAS a grifter. He worked for a top-flight talent agency on Wilshire Boulevard, but the job was secured for him through the influence of his wife's relations, and people acquainted with his circumstances understood it was window dressing; although, for that matter, how many instances are there where parents, quietly and behind the scenes, make this sort of accommodation for their sons-in-law. He was ex-pro football player, one of those sports celebrities to be seen at the clubs and gatherings around town, the nature of the community being what it was. He had courted the young daughter of an extremely wealthy family, had married her, and the family found the place for him at the agency so that he would have something to do and keep occupied.

The agency used him as a leg man in the field—because he was personable and a former athlete and so had something to trade on, and because he wasn't much good to them in any other capacity. His job essentially was to move around with the stars on the list and in this way give them the feeling they were being worried about; but in the case of Adele Hogue it had gone further than that. He had taken up with her, had gotten into her good graces, slept with her. Claris was no better than most. She was accessible. She was on the rebound, just back from England, the latest of her marriages having collapsed on her. She was a big name, one of the handful who really brought people into the movie house. Claris had been with the agency long enough to know what a personality like Hogue meant in the business; he wasn't unaffected by her standing and importance, knew how useful a connection with her could be; and so, with the opportunity presenting itself, he had gone ahead. Now she was creating a major disturbance. In a fit or fury, she had run away from the picture she was shooting in, had driven out to this hotel-resort in the desert, leaving everything at a standstill, the production schedule completely disrupted—and Claris was trapped in the heart of the upset. Dick Prescott, the senior man on the assignment and the one properly in charge, called him straight out to the hotel as soon as the crisis broke, and was turning the whole responsibility over to him. When Claris caught up with his associate, it was down at the hotel parking lot. Prescott was already on his way to his car, hurrying to duck out.

"That's what you get for schtuppin with the talent, you're stuck," Prescott said. He was a slick, easy-rolling individual, a bachelor at the present time, his mind on motels and the after-hours rat race, and he was in this testy, distracted mood, not so much on account of Hogue and the commotion but because he was having trouble with the chippies lately, a standup just the night before. "Ever since television," he said. "They can all get some kind of a jerk job, dancing, or else just standing around, acting, and I tell you it's rough."

Claris didn't like the idea of having the whole load thrust on his shoulders. He was out of his depth. It was too much for him. The actress was tying up an expensive production. Hard losses could result. She was an intense, unstable bundle of a woman, with a long record of excesses behind her, periodically in the papers with her marriages and tantrums, and there was no telling to what extremes she might go or what could happen.

"True, true," Prescott said, as Claris stood parleying with him in the sun. "But what could I do with her? What could anybody in the office do? You're the logical choice. You're in solid with her and I'm only getting out of the way so you can have a free hand." That was what he would tell them at the agency if they came at him later on with a beef. He wanted to stay as far away from the mess as he could get.

"Nice for you. You've got it all worked out," Claris said.

"That's right," Prescott said.

"If anything goes wrong, I'm the heavy."

"Why should I jeopardize myself? You knew what you were doing when you started up with her, now take the consequences. Do it, do it. Ride it out," Prescott said, brushing him off and moving around the front of the car. "Nothing'll happen. Sooner or later they get sick of it. She'll simmer down. She'll go back to the studio and that'll be the end of it." He got the car into gear, backed out, and Claris was left alone, fretting and uncertain in the heavy heat.

He was in an awkward position. He had to tread carefully. He couldn't afford to take chances with his in-laws, his wife's parents, her uncles and brothers, the whole clan, and get mixed up in a scandal, and considering the relationship he had fallen into with the actress, he was wide open. He didn't know what to do, how to proceed. Adele Hogue had one of the outside bungalows that were spaced around the main building; she wasn't in the hotel itself. Claris had looked up a Filipino steward he knew on the place, had had the bungalow pointed out to him when he had arrived, so he knew which one she was in, and he started out now, thinking he would go up and see her.

The hotel-resort lay in the Palm Springs area, that is to say, for the sake of those not familiar with this section of the country, in that heavily promoted desert real-estate development a hundred miles southeast of Los Angeles on the freeways. It was patronized, naturally, by rich people, not necessarily in the movie business— all kinds, from all over. They were people getting on in years, shunning the limelight and seasoned, the women the second and third wives of men who made big money

6

in meat, oil, or textiles. The men had their offices in St. Louis, in Chicago, in cities in Texas, and since they or their wives insisted on living on the West Coast, they were constantly obliged to be in transit, commuting from point to point. The husbands, those who were coming out this morning, were still on the freeways, driving in from the airports in Los Angeles, and when Claris emerged from the parking lot, there were few couples about, just a scattering of guests, mainly women, lolling in the sun and chatting.

The grounds stretched hushed, everything spick-and-span and burning, so early in the morning. Claris didn't feel at home with these people. He knew he didn't belong with them and that he was on his own. He kept away from them, taking a circuitous route to the actress's cottage, sticking to the edges of the grounds, and as he went on, he suddenly came around a bend in the path and saw a couple straight ahead, the woman very well cared for and beautiful, the husband so-so. Claris held up. The couple weren't aware they were being observed. "Sexy figure, Sid," the wife said, nudging her husband, indicating a guest not far off in a playsuit. It was as though she was appraising the guest for his benefit, and Sid, the husband, dourly inspected the guest and chomped his cigar.

"You ought to see her in the morning when she gets out of bed in her nightgown," he said.

Claris didn't stir, lingering in the shade to give the couple time to move on. He was on the grift and had been on the grift practically since his college days, but, remarkably, his way of life hadn't hardened him. He remembered the plane trips after the game, when he was still playing ball; he remembered how he used to sit in the gloom on those homeward trips, whether they had won or lost, hurting from the beatings he had to take, wondering what would happen to him after he was through and they didn't want him around any more. He had worked his luck, had gotten himself into the favored clubs and dining rooms, had listened to the smart money talk to be heard in those glossy, comfortable places: "The rich get wrinkles only from smiling." "I've been poor, I've been rich—believe me, being rich is better." It hadn't turned out for him as he thought it would. Everything stayed remote. The smart money talk didn't apply to him. His wife's folks had all kinds of money— a West Coast chain of supermarkets, together with the real estate and financing that went with such an operation, the subsidiary interests by this time easily accounting for the larger share of their wealth. But the money had nothing to do with him. Very little of it came his way. The family bought Claris and his wife a home; they provided servants, a nurse for the baby when the child came along; they fixed him up with the job. Claris trooped to the different studios with his agent's black book, working at his bogus, makeshift job. He was consistently unfaithful to his young, inexperienced wife. He didn't know why he did these things, why he seemed compelled to do them, or why he seemed determined to get himself into the hot, sticky impasses his infidelities invariably led to. "Maybe everything would be all right if only she wasn't so rich," he mused aloud, killing a half hour in some office as he made his rounds at the studios. He tried to put the blame on that, on the heavy money standing there all the time in the background behind her. "She's sweet. She's simple. I could love her. We should be happy. Of course," he said, frowning and shifting, "if it wasn't for the money, if it wasn't for the supermarkets and the holding companies, I wouldn't be there, would I?" His mother came visiting at his lavish home on Sundays and sat at the poolside with the baby in her lap, her eyes silently pleading—she needed money. The man she had married didn't work, and Claris seesawed with her painfully, giving her most of the three hundred a week he earned at the agency. He was bothered by his debasement. He was mortified by his mother's half-hearted visits, by his wrangles with her, by the incredible way in which he openly talked about his troubles to people he met in studio offices. And wherever he went, at the back of his neck he waited for the cry to ring out: "Stop thief!"

WHEN HE GOT into the room with her at the cottage, she was in a black slip, fighting with her daughter Melanie, a lumpish child of ten, with thick-lensed glasses, who was sitting in a corner waiting for the harangue to be over with so that she could get on with the book she was reading. The actress had two other children beside Melanie, a set of twins by a later, also unsuccessful marriage. As she stood in her slip berating the child, she held an armful of combs and brushes which she was evidently in the process of cleaning at this time. She looked up at Claris, over the heap of combs and brushes, and shot him a hard, angry glance, either because she resented his intrusion or else because she had been waiting for him and he had been slow in coming, Claris didn't know which.

"What did they do, send you down to chastise me?" she asked. "What do you think you're going to be able to accomplish?"

Claris gave her to understand he wasn't acting as an

agent, that he hadn't made the trip solely for business purposes. "I don't know what you get by running away and driving people crazy," he said. "Are you planning to stay cooped up for the rest of your life? You're going to have to come out some day." The bolt had caught him by surprise. He hadn't known anything about the disturbance until he heard from Prescott. "Why didn't you at least call me before you took off?"

"Because I didn't want to do it that way," she said. "Because I wanted you to come flying to me of your own volition. Don't you know, we crave attention. They say when you're with one of us, you have to stop living and do nothing but worry about our problems."

The drapes were pulled together at the windows, but the lights were turned on and there was a hothouse, unnatural glare in the room—the lights all burning at ten o'clock in the morning. Claris saw there was no point in tackling her head on, so he settled himself in the hot bath of light, waiting on her and letting her give forth— which was probably what she wanted him there for, he supposed—and it became an arduous, drawn-out vigil, the child sitting in the room with them, keeping her nose buried in the book but not missing a trick.

The times he and the actress had been together had been mean, furtive sessions, afternoons snatched on the run and under pressure—they were times when she should have been on the set, when he had gone after her, ostensibly to argue with her and wheedle her down to the sound-stages; and in the heat of those stealthy sessions

11

together, Claris—who was on edge and flustered enough as it was with his own misgivings, not quite sure of what he was taking on—had never known how to contend with the nutty-putty ball of despair that he had with her. He didn't know what to make of her. She was a main-eventer, a true box-office money star—Claris knew you could walk into any studio with just her name on a contract and make your own deal, and it was this consideration, no doubt, in the back of his mind somewhere, that had led him to start up with her in the first place and ingratiate himself with her. She had lived through big things—the many marriages, children by different husbands, this last marriage in England to a marquis or lord, the son of a famous, highly publicized sporting duke—but when he was in the room with her, it was startling how little there was to her. She was ordinary, immature, smaller and slighter, as they all seemed off screen, altogether incapable of surmounting the difficulties that were be-setting her. She couldn't get on with the picture. She couldn't make it to the set. It was one of those pictures with the crickets chirping all the way through on the sound track. She had to walk around in flat-heeled shoes in the part, and she didn't know what to do with herself, she didn't know what was expected of her. She couldn't stand the gray mourning doves outside her hotel in Beverly Hills, the way they groaned and gurgled. She couldn't stand the commercial planes rattling overhead one after the other these days like freight cars in the sky. People's faces suddenly seemed strange to her; there was something about the eyes, the eyes were speckled—even the faces she saw on television. She was worried about the vertical ridges on her fingernails; she read Dr. Alvarez in the morning paper, and Dr. Alvarez, or somebody like him, said the vertical ridges meant the root ends of your nerves inside you were fraying and giving out. Together with her hallucinations and caprices, she was filled with that raw, unmanageable grievance they had, that wholesale complaint and rebellion. They were in demand, always fiddled with, diddled, sweet-talked, misused and betrayed, and when they had something troubling them, this festering, senseless belligerence was the only way they seemed to know of fending for themselves. She was eaten up with the fiasco of her English marriage. That was at the bottom of the emotional turmoil she was going through, of the outcries and wild fights; but there had been other upheavals, other fiascos, other causes. She had sailed off in style a year and a half ago, starting out on her grand new life—and now it was eighteen months later and everything was a savage comedown for her, a humiliating torment.

"People are so persnickety. They all think they have dibs on you," she said. She was taking out in her misery after the sightseers and hangers-on, those wealthy women guests at the hotel who preferred the life on the West Coast and hovered on the fringes of the movie scene. "Everybody around here is so broad-beamed and phlegmatic. They lay there with their aplomb, getting their perfect, even suntans. They think they've got it all solved.

It seems the only enjoyment people can get out of life is to look down on you and be superior. Why don't you go out of doors and play for five minutes?" she said, turning on Melanie, afflicted now by the child's unfortunate appearance, by the thick glasses and the roly-poly awkwardness. "Why don't you take care of the twins?" The twins were boys, four or five years younger than Melanie.

"But I don't know where they are," Melanie said, stolid, holding fast.

"Find them, look for them. That's the whole idea. It wouldn't do you harm to be active and lose some weight. Sticks to me like glue," she said, breaking off. "She sits like a bump on a log, reading and ruining her eyesight, and I can't get her off my head. I don't even have ammonia," she said, embittered. She needed the ammonia for the combs and brushes. Ammonia was the only thing. "It just goes to show," she said, "the lousy, unsatisfactory way I live—I don't even have the most common, ordinary, everyday household articles when I need them."

Claris didn't know why she was chipping away at the fashionable women guests outside or why she had to come here if these strangers annoyed her so. He didn't know what was beating up in her, why she was so agitated. Prescott had said she would simmer down, that sooner or later they got sick of the commotions they raised, but there was no sign of a letup in her. The slip hiked up on her legs as she carried on, as she came flaring at Claris with her complaints about the bottle of ammonia which she needed and didn't have, and he saw the flash of the flesh at her thighs, he saw the breasts pulling and quivering there at the top of the slip, and he wondered at the stark force and energy of the turbulence in her. Generally they had a bosom companion with them to tide them over a bad spell—a favorite hairdresser, somebody from casting—but she was all alone, nobody with her but the child, nobody to turn to but Claris himself, and suddenly it struck him—he was the bosom companion. That was why she wanted him near her. That was why she had succumbed and fallen into his arms. He was the one who was getting taken, not the other way around.

She was sitting on the edge of the wash basin in the bathroom, the water running over the combs and brushes in the basin, while in the meantime she worked carefully at the medicine-chest mirror on her eye makeup, penciling in the dark smeary stuff under the lids. She was running water over the combs and brushes instead of soaking them in the ammonia she needed because she wouldn't call the desk for ammonia—because it was too much trouble, because she didn't want to ask, because she had no patience. The shopping she had to do brought on a similar convulsion of feeling, a similar flurry, and it was ultimately the clue that took Claris to the heart of the difficulty. That was why she was in the black slip—she was preparing, in her own time, to get dressed and go out to the shops. She needed clothes; she had nothing to wear; she didn't know anybody at the shops in Palm Springs or where to go; but again she backed and fussed. Again she wouldn't bestir herself. She didn't want the hotel to set up appointments for her. She didn't want to make a hullabaloo. She wasn't going to call on Fannie Case and let her do favors for her, and then it came to Claris—with the mention of Fannie Case's name, the pieces fell into place in his mind. It wasn't the stylish ladies at the resort who were upsetting the actress. It was Harry Case, Fannie Case's former husband. Fannie Case owned the hotel; she was the proprietor and manager of the place. It was an old story, an excitement in the papers at the time and still a recurring blind item now and then in the columns. Harry Case was, or had been, an operator in the gambling rackets—slot machines, horse-betting syndicates, Eastern connections, as Claris recalled. It had all happened in the days not long after the war, when the people came flocking out to California, when the boom began. Adele Hogue had gone a furious, fast few rounds with him. The romance hadn't lasted— Adele had soon left him high and dry—but it was enough to break up the Cases' marriage, and, in the peculiar, illogical way of these things, it ended—as Claris should have remembered—with the three of them knit together on a continuing, more or less permanent basis, Fannie becoming friends with the star and Harry hankering after her. He carried the torch. He kept interfering in her doings, taking an interest in her welfare and never letting go—and with the crisis she had made for herself by bolting the picture and coming to the hotel, he now had a royal, heaven-sent chance to move in on her again.

She had balked at the production calls morning after

16

morning. It was a kind of paralysis that immobilized her
—they still had the first foot of film on her to photo-
graph. "You lose interest. Nobody likes to do anything
all of the time," she had once told Claris, tossing and re-
sisting and defending herself. "You stand in front of
them—the electricians, the cameramen, the director. You
don't know what to do. There is nothing there. You are
nothing. You feel guilty. You feel like the worst criminal
in the world." Out of the blue, in some spasm of determination or contrition, she had abruptly decided to make
peace with the company; she had given assurances that
she was ready to work, that she had herself under control
and would appear on the set positively and without fail.
And then when the deadline came on and the paralysis
seized hold again, when she physically couldn't get herself to the set, she couldn't just sit there in her shame at
the hotel in Beverly Hills. She had to do something, so
she had grabbed the children and gone running to Fannie. That was how it had happened. But from her point
of view, it was the worst possible thing she could have
done. Claris stared at her, befuddled. It was as though
she had deliberately gone looking for trouble. She had
made the grandstand play at the time of her marriage,
saying goodbye to the movies for good, practically blowing kisses to the crowds; she was home in disgrace now,
forced to pick up her career again, forced to face the
music, and the mere sight of Case would be a mocking,
infuriating reminder, bringing back every indignity and
defeat.

17

"What did you think would happen when you came here?" Claris asked. "Didn't you realize he'd only come chasing after you? Did you want him here?"

"But where else did I have to go?" she said to him. She had no family. She had no friends. Fannie was the only person she knew. "You think you can just get up and go? You have to go somewhere!"

"But what good is it? What sense does it make? What are you going to do, hide out here and fight with Case and in the meantime the whole picture goes to pieces and everything gets ruined?" He tried to explain to her that a sizable investment was at stake, that jobs and livelihoods depended on the production. But she was beyond caring about the picture. She came tumbling at him with those doctored, golliwog eyes, raging and pouring out her resentment, and he pulled up and quit.

"The way they come out at you with the digs," she said. She meant the agents. "They give you the business, nodding and agreeing, making out they're attending to your every little whim, and all the time they're getting in their weasel shots—how it's a national disaster to walk out on a picture, how they can sue you for millions. I don't know why the studios don't pay you the commission. That's who you do the work for, not us."

"Mother, the water is running," Melanie said, from her corner. "Mother, you left the water running. It could overflow."

"The only thing is to be strong," the actress said. "Nobody will ever help you. You have to do it yourself.

You can wait until the cows come home. Everybody is concerned only with their own self-interest."

She walked away to take care of the combs and brushes. The room became quiet. Melanie returned to her book, smoothing the skirt of her dress over her knees, and in another moment Claris could see Adele there on her perch on the wash basin, applying her eye makeup at the medicine-chest mirror.

THE WOMEN WERE OUT in force on the terrace. The day was wearing on. The actress's cottage lay off to the side by itself in the sun, all that havoc and ruin going on within, but here at the main building of the hotel, thirty or forty yards away, the life of the resort was following its usual course. There was the swirl of action, the rise of voices, the women sitting at the different tables in their friendly clusters, passing the time among themselves, and as Claris came by, he could hear fragments of the conversation, bits of the patter and gossip. The women guests knew what was happening with Hogue—the news was all over the place —but these cataclysms, these runaways and panics, weren't infrequent in the business, and the women took them, when they came along, with a decent restraint. Claris didn't particularly care to be with the crowd, but he hadn't much choice. There was no other place for him to go. He couldn't leave the premises; the agency wanted at least one man there all the time. It was almost confounding how strung up and imprisoned he was by the realities of his predicament. He hadn't been able to stay locked in forever with the actress, while she stewed and fussed and endlessly prepared to go shopping, so he had slipped out of the bungalow some time ago, had wandered over the grounds, and now found himself on the terrace, like an impostor or sneak thief on the prowl, part of the social hubbub and the company, whether he wanted or didn't want to be with them. He paused at the edge of the tables, taking up a position between the terrace and the hotel lobby from which it extended, so that he could look out on both areas, and as he loitered at this position, the voices of the women at the adjoining table reached him. They were talking about garter fasteners, garter clasps, the difficulties they had in finding the right kind. "It's such a nuisance, always having the old fasteners to sew on," a woman in the group was saying; she preferred the flat buckles, not the ones with the little knobs that showed through the dress, and every time she bought a new girdle, she said, she had to go through the inconvenience of transferring the fasteners. "Strange to say, the salesgirls all tell me that flat buckles aren't popular, no one wants them," the woman said.

Bearing down in Claris's direction, making her way through the guests and calling out greetings to them, surrounded by a covey of her assistants, was the proprietor of the hotel, Fannie Case. Claris had stopped off a few moments on his wanderings to check with Louis, the Filipino steward he knew on the place. Louis had mentioned the hotel owner would be there—that was probably one of the reasons which had led Claris to the terrace. She was an old-timer; her fingers were covered with diamond rings, large stones, and her white hair was blued. This was her busy time of day. By rights she should have been down in the kitchen—she had the ordering to supervise, the cooks to talk to—but instead she was out on the floor, doing her work in this makeshift manner with her assistants, because she wanted to be close to the desk in the lobby and on hand when her former husband arrived. As nearly as Claris could make out, Harry Case was being held up by a tieup on the freeway. Louis had heard the radio Sigalert, the police call advising motorists—those, that is, who still hadn't entered the freeway—to choose alternate routes to their destination where possible. They had these great jams on the freeways. Normally the traffic drummed ahead in its furor, the cars careening at sixty-five miles an hour or more over the four-lane sweep of the freeway; but when an accident occurred, a collision or breakdown, the cars piled up in a fearful chain reaction, slamming into one another and hurtling themselves all over the hard, concrete roadbed, blocking the four lanes, and then the traffic backed up for miles and the whole roaring maelstrom came to a halt. It took a long time to clear the wreckage after one of these crashes, to send the miles of stalled cars speeding again, and so Mrs. Case was now on the terrace, bustling and hooting to the guests, attending to her work on the move, while she waited for her ex-husband to show up.

Claris didn't want to draw attention to himself. His idea was to keep under cover, to do everything he could to avoid being publicly associated with the case. His wife was out of town, as it happened, on a visit with Eastern relatives, with her grandparents, and he had a certain leeway as far as she was concerned, at least for the time being; but there were his in-laws to think of, the brothers and the uncles, and he didn't know who there might be in this crowd who could give him away and make trouble for him if anything broke. Everybody knew everybody, people liked to talk, and you could always count on the word getting through where it would do the most damage. Claris hoped the hotel owner would sweep by with her entourage and not notice him; but also on the terrace, roving through the guests, was the producer of the picture, Robert Wigler. The producer had a heavy weight on him, his sets standing idle in Culver City, the overhead mounting, and the actress here in Palm Springs, intransigent. He was ensconced at the hotel, waiting on events, without too much to do, and when he spied Claris, he walked over—to discuss the situation, to confer. Mrs. Case saw him, and promptly came surging forward, the assistants bobbing along after her. She set herself up on the spot with Wigler and Claris, speaking out and unburdening herself, riffling through the invoices from the supply houses, and they became a threesome, a social cluster of their own, in full, open view of everyone. "Not so glamorous," she said, harsh and oblivious, referring to the star.

She was wound up, all excited by the emergency. It was a long-standing relationship between her and Adele, dating back, as Claris knew, to the scandal. According to the stories, Fannie had never had anything against the actress from the beginning. She was too hardheaded and practical to be able to blame the breakup of her marriage on the younger woman. So they had fallen in together in the unusual aftermath. Fannie became the confidante, the guide. An attachment grew up over the years. Adele Hogue invariably went straight to Fannie's when she was in trouble, and now Fannie had the whole upset deposited in her lap, the ménage with the three small children, the strife, and her ex-husband coming up in a rush too. "Every time you see the twins, they're running around the lobby like two little rats, peeking into the Ladies' Room," Fannie said. Claris didn't know how well she knew Wigler, but she was a direct individual, with no nonsense to her, and she let go freely with whatever was on her mind. "She is all girl, always looking for love—'At last, at last, I have found the one man who can interest me romantically.'" She was mimicking the actress's words, referring to all the liaisons, to the many marriages, to this last one which was responsible for the turmoil now. "She goes shooting off, seeking the bluebird of happiness, and then I'm the one who has to pick up the pieces. I'm the patsy." Mrs.

Case knew about the shopping the actress intended to do. "She lays there in the dumps, all tuckered out and exhausted, neglects the children and diets, and then suddenly her clothes don't fit and she starts hollering she needs a whole new wardrobe." Hogue had a driver with her at the hotel—the driver was on call for the trip into Palm Springs—and it was comparatively easy for Mrs. Case to know what the actress was up to by checking with the chauffeur.

Not far from where they were standing, in the dimness of the lobby, a man—one of the husbands who commuted to the resort and who had just pulled in—was having a heated, deeply felt argument with his wife. The husband had beaten the pack, scrambling over the alternate routes, and in his haste and anxiety, frazzled by the traffic delay, by the hard ride over the country side roads, he had pitched into his wife right then and there, his voice coming over in a steady, muted cataract. The diversion nettled Mrs. Case.

"Too damned inconsiderate and carried away to go upstairs to the room and fight in private like they should," she said, thrown offstride and crowded by the marital quarrel. "I wouldn't give you five cents for all them big-hit, rich-guy marriages put together. What do you expect, they're no dummies." She was referring to the husbands. "Deep down they know the wife's got nothing but contempt for them, and it's a Donnybrook, cat and dog from the word go." She looked up, saw Claris watching her, and took a moment for him. "You the feller from the agency? It's a dilly—make yourself at home." She meant the whole eruption with Hogue, the crisis, and that they wouldn't be getting through with it so fast.

The women at the adjoining tables stirred in the chairs, glancing over their shoulders at the couple in the hall. The women commented on the fracas.

"What is it, she has a fetish—a hundred and eight dollars for stockings?" That was what the husband was clamoring at his wife about, among other things, that she was spending too much, that she was heedless and uncaring.

"No, no. Not at one time. Over the year, over the year."

"He adds it up?"

"Well, he's dipping into capital," the second woman said, the one who had corrected the first speaker. "He's having troubles, I don't know—business, taxes."

Her voice trailed, and in the lull the voice of the husband came over, sharp and maddened. "You got an idea the kind of money it costs nowadays to send a person through medical college?" He was meeting the bills for her younger brother's education, it appeared. "And what about your mother," he went on, "blackmailing us, threatening to take us into court for non-support, the three hundred a month I give her not enough to suit her?"

"Good, good," Mrs. Case said, taking a vicious delight in the husband's outburst, in his discomfiture. She was the first wife, so to speak, and Claris could well understand the rancor in her. He could see why she was so aroused or enlivened, and what the present situation meant to her. "These old fools with the pots," she said, scribbling on the invoices, "the minute they accumulate a lousy few hundred thousand dollars, right away they're off to the races. They can't wait, it burns in them, they got to get themselves a jazzy looker, and then boom, doubts, recriminations—the wife don't reciprocate enough." She had had the bad years in New York with Case, when he was bruising his way up to the top, full of power and muscle in those days, mixing with the rough element in the gambling rackets. She had had the grief and worry, as Claris had heard, hunting for Case at the Turkish baths, at the hotels in the Catskills, when he had disappeared from sight; and then when they had finally made it, when they came out to California to live, he had gone dancing off without a by-your-leave, putting on the big show, monkeying with movie stars, and it hurt, for all her broadmindedness and tolerance and toughness. She wasn't made of stone, and it was a kind of victory, a tingling retribution, everything coming home to roost with her—after all, it was her hotel. She owned the place. "Good!" she trumpeted, finishing with her work, shoving the papers over to her assistants. "They wanted a showgirl for a wife, then let them suffer. Let them see the belly doctors. Let them go to Cedars with nervous exhaustion." She turned to a guest sunning herself there some steps away on a chaise. "Hey, Debbie," she hallooed, invigorated, "the gams are holding out great—who gives you shots?"

She shooed the kitchen help away, sending them back

to their jobs, and then made her excuses to Wigler and Claris—she had to talk a little Turkish to the Mexican chambermaids, she said. "See you later." She wheeled about, went marching off into the lobby, soon dwindled in the distance, in the screen of passers-by, and Claris was left alone with the producer. Cedars of Lebanon, of course, was the big hospital in Hollywood.

In the lobby, the husband broke away from his wife; the cataract ceased. Claris could see the face of the man as he went tearing past, ravaged and grim. The woman on the chaise, the one Mrs. Case had addressed, was getting ready to go in—somebody was calling her name. She sat up on the chaise, hovered a moment, and looked at her legs. "Another two years, three at the most, and then goodbye," she said, more to herself than to anyone near her. "Coming, coming," she called. She got to her feet, straightened her blouse, her shorts, and started sliding between the tables. Claris was pinned down; as a matter of courtesy, since he was a representative of the agency, he was obliged to stand by and humor the producer. Wigler was aware that Claris was a minor employee and of no importance, but he nevertheless rambled on at length, subdued, suspended. There was nothing to be done and he had to fill in the time somehow. He was a man deep into middle age, with a portly, deliberate bearing and dignity. He was ruminating on the star, on the personal difficulties she found herself in and the situation now with the Cases. He knew as well as Claris did how enmeshed she was, how benighted and defenseless, and that any imbroglio with Case would bring on more distress, more altercation and disorder.

"Psychologically it's a severe readjustment for her, a traumatic shock, and under the best of conditions, as we know, they're insecure," he commented, dry, making allowances. He had been through the mill himself, dealing with stars, with the banks and the daily crises of motion picture production, and he had a ready, resigned acceptance of human nature and its oddities. "Did you go in? Were you with her?" he asked Claris, but when Claris started to say something about his visit and the state he had found her in, the producer shrugged and looked away. It was as he expected. The bolt caught him at an acute, critical juncture. He was actually under great pressure. His immediate concerns had to do with the intricacies of motion-picture financing, with the end money —the cash with which to begin a picture and to complete it, at both ends. There were such things as completion bonds to be posted, the banks made rigid requirements; Wigler had set dates to meet and was seriously off balance.

"I don't know how they have the strength even to think up all the different, complicated involvements they get themselves into," he said, "but they do. It seems they go out of their way intentionally looking for headaches. People are unhappy," he continued. "You want to know why? Simple. I'll tell you. Time passes. We wear out. Life disappoints us. Not only movie stars. Everyone. You'd be surprised, don't laugh, but there are people walking in the streets every day in the week who are stark, raving crazy, only we don't know."

Claris had to hold tight. He had to pay deference, clucking along and sagely nodding his head, trying at all costs to keep matter of fact and cool. Wigler had no notion Claris was personally messed up with the actress, and Claris was anxious to give no sign. And as he held tight, nodding and agreeing, at the same time his eyes constantly veered to the lobby. He was searching for Fannie Case. He had lost track of her. He was puzzled, uneasy—she was obviously bent on meeting her former husband as he arrived, and yet she had gone marching clear off the floor to talk to the chambermaids somewhere. Claris didn't know how he was going to be able to recognize Case when he appeared. Louis had promised to tip him off as soon as Case drove in, but Louis was badly rushed with the guests today, receiving them and settling them down, the arrivals disorganized because of the freeway tieup, and Claris doubted that the steward would be able to get away.

The producer was gone, no longer standing alongside. He had finished with his observations, or had tired and lost interest, and had drawn off without notice or ceremony. Claris could see him pushing out among the guests, and just at that moment, as he cast about to pick up Wigler in the swirl, out of the corner of his eye he glimpsed Mrs. Case in the lobby again. She had turned up out of nowhere and was moving fast toward the desk, toward a man there, a single arrival, Case.

Claris waited a moment, letting Wigler get out of range, and then gingerly maneuvered himself down to the desk. People were coming and going. Claris had to take pains to make it not seem that he was eavesdropping, and as he dawdled in the area, keeping aloof and pretending he was waiting for someone to come down and join him, the interchange between the Cases carried across to him in hot, disjointed bursts and snatches. The two of them were rattling away, lost and embroiled, standing together under an arch to the side of the reception desk. "Shopping? Shopping?" Case said, hard-ridden, perplexed, and then Claris heard Fannie singing out: "How should I know what goes on in her head?" Case had apparently asked about Hogue, wanting to know what she was doing, and Fannie apparently had told him. Case was low-slung, pugnacious, with a prize-fighter's stance and truculence, the hurry and stress of the moment putting a homely crimp to his features, and Claris could hear Fannie chipping at him, looking him over. "What's new in Vegas?" she said, mocking, giving him none of the best of it. "The faces go lopsided and start falling apart. He's got a mirror in his apartment there which shows him he has a full head of hair and still looks good."

"Boy, you step out of line with them and they got it on you for the rest of your life," Case said. He had reached the place some minutes ago and had evidently been kept waiting by the desk clerk until Fannie could get to him and go to work on him. He was used up, out of temper from the hours in the desert heat, from the tieup. He wanted a room. He wanted a shower. "She's burned out," he said, grating, meaning Adele. "Them cookies go good so long as it's unconscious. The minute they get on to themselves, they're through. The flop sweat comes crawling out on her and she starts shaking in her boots."

"What are you yammering at me for?" Fannie said, indignant. "What am I got to do with it?"

"She got down on her hands and knees, apologizing to beat the band, making a first-class sap out of herself, and then when the showdown came, nothing—the same as before." Claris winced as the image came back to him. Case was referring to the scene Hogue had made, to the impulsive, deluded act of contrition that had misfired and sent her driving out to the resort. What she had done, in her derangement, was to go out to the set. She had faced the whole company, the cast and crew, on that bare, hushed sound-stage—demeaning herself without stint, saying how unprofessional her conduct was. She had promised with all her heart that she would make amends, that she would be the first one on the set the following morning and that henceforth all would go well.

Their voices fell low. They were huddled in tight, going round and round now, and Claris had to steal up closer in order to catch the drift of what they were saying. Fannie was driving away in earnest. She was trying to head Case off, to keep him away from Adele, telling him his presence on the scene would only aggravate the problem. Case fought back, shunting aside her arguments, not wanting to hear them, and it impressed Claris, even as they intently bickered and belabored each other, that there was still a peculiar bond between them, an old-time intimacy and rapport.

"You want to let her go straight down the drain?" Case demanded. Somebody had to take hold, he said. Somebody had to put her back on the rails. "This ain't the old days. They'll throw her right out on her keister. There's the kids to be protected. You think of that? What about the kids in the middle?"

"You'll be the one who'll save the situation? You're the champion? Tell the truth, Harry," she said, blunt and unsparing, "every time she got a divorce, didn't you get a sense of satisfaction out of it? Didn't you go running Johnnie-on-the-Spot?"

"What's that got to do with it?" Case asked. "What are you bringing that up for? Who wants her? It's the kids."

"Who are you trying to fool?" Fannie said. "Don't I know you from the old days? Don't I know you better than you know yourself? You were star crazy then and you're still star crazy. You saw your chance and you came busting all over yourself. You can't wait to get your fingers on her."

"For my part she can go walking out into the ocean until her hat floats," Case said, crashing down, bringing the argument to a finish once for all, and from where Claris was standing at the wall, remembering to remain hidden, he could feel the hard force in the man, the anger and exasperation. "Fannie, don't stand me on my head. You don't know anything about it. Whatever she has to do, she'll do. Just let me handle it. Lords and dukes," he seethed. "The phonies we got here weren't flashy enough for her. She had to go for that international jet-set bull and marry this English foul ball with the racing stables."

"The language is very nice," Fannie said, seeing it was a lost cause. Case wasn't turning around and going back. "That's all we need, a few refined expressions out of your vocabulary."

"Am I making it up? It's not the truth? She heard about them pansies all going over there and she had to get a whiff of it too—Monte Carlo and all them ritzy foreign places with the lousy plumbing." He had gone after her, wanting her, carrying the torch, as the saying went, whatever carrying the torch meant with these people, and she had steadfastly kept knocking him down. She had gotten away from him altogether—eighteen months out of the country with the European crowd— and now that she was on the skids and he had her back again, wild horses weren't going to stop him. "Bunch of no-good parasites and free-loaders, the whole crummy bunch of them," he said. "Who are they? Have they got a pot or a window to throw it out of, any single one of them?"

"For crying out loud, have a heart, Harry—there's people passing!"

"What did I say?" He caught himself. He saw what

he had said. "If they never heard it before, then they won't know what I'm talking about. If they know what it means, then what have they got to be so chintzy about? What do you have to do around here to get a room?" he said. "You going to let me stay in the lobby all day?"

"Give him the room," Fannie said to the desk clerk. The boy was rattled, fumbled the job at the keyboard, and it ended with Fannie going around the counter herself. "That puts the lid on it," she said, fed up, disgusted. "She'll take one look at you and goodbye Charlie. Now we got it. She comes here, a woman at the end of her rope with three small children on her hands, always impractical, too goddam big to bother with alimony— not like these prostitutes here."

"I should tip my hat to her?" Case said.

"Big shot!" Fannie said. "She insulted his ego and committed the crime of the century!"

"She's in no bed of roses." Case had himself in control again and was standing at the desk while Fannie went through the business of booking him into the hotel. He'd get at Adele as soon as he cleaned up, he said, shopping or no shopping—she could change her mind and go shopping some other time. "One thing about these kewpie dolls, they always boomerang on themselves. Cripes, they never know how to win."

"The room's not ready. You'll have to wait until they make it up," Fannie said to him. "Don't even know how to buy." She was back on Adele again. "In New York one time she stayed petrified in the hotel suite, too scared of her shadow to go out. 'For Chrissake,' I told her, 'call Ceil Chapman, call Bonwit's. They'll send up a raft of dresses—you'll pick and choose.' But no, she couldn't budge herself—no moxie in her, no energy."

But she was talking to herself. It was over. Case had taken the key off the desk, had picked up his bag, and was waddling down to the room—he knew the way and didn't require a bellboy to carry his bag for him. Fannie busied herself behind the desk for a while, bossing the clerk around. Then her heels went tapping on the floor tiles, the tapping faded away, and Claris was released.

The hotel was built on a rise of ground, the kitchen lying on a lower level, to the back of and under the structure. Claris was going around the side of the hotel, getting away from the lobby, when he was unexpectedly brought to a stop by Louis, the steward. There was a kind of hollow leading down to the kitchen entrance, and Louis, standing at the kitchen door, called to him. Louis assumed that by this time Claris was aware of Case's presence on the grounds; what he was waiting to tell Claris about was the news of a man they knew, a singer or actor named Pepi Straeger, who had just been killed in a car crash. Dealing with the guests as they came in off the freeway, Louis had been able to get word of the accident. Pepi Straeger was a hanger-on, a fixture at the social gatherings at homes and tennis clubs, a Viennese singer who had once been fairly successful in operettas, in revues, but who had fallen on bad days, his style of singing having years ago gone out of favor. Claris had seen him around, pushing his luck—jockeying cars for people, making himself handy, hunting up bit acting parts—and it was a disagreeable shock to hear now of his sudden death. Louis couldn't say whether it was actually this accident that had caused the freeway jam, but if it wasn't this accident, then Straeger had met his death in another accident, occurring down the line on some other stretch of the road, at another time; or else, as sometimes happened, there were two accidents, separate and yet related, both of them contributing to and causing the traffic pileup.

Louis was taking a break, having a smoke outside the kitchen entrance between errands, and Claris stayed with him there, lost in a train of thought about the singer and his passing. Straeger had lately been in the foreground. He had some months ago linked himself to a woman with a really substantial fortune, a patent medicine company whose product was a household name. It was a big coup, a stroke on the grand scale, but Straeger had managed it—the wedding was announced—and Claris didn't know whether the accident, coming just then, was a portent, an admonition, or whether it came with no meaning at all. Louis lingered alongside, with his reticence, with his way of making a little stunt out of smoking a cigarette, exhaling in fine, discreet slants. He was slight of build, a Filipino, his hair thinning evenly over his scalp, and he held himself with a stiff reserve. He had a deep, respectful regard for Claris, admiring him for his physique, for his athletic prowess, for the celebrity of his marriage—an admiration that Claris could do without. Claris didn't want his solicitude or respectful regard. Louis understood all about Hogue and the awkward position Claris was in right now with the actress, and he wondered whether the accident of Straeger's would bring on more complications. "Will they want you to go down and take care of things?" Louis said, murmuring, keeping his distance. He meant the agency. He mistakenly thought Straeger was a client of the agency.

"No, he's not one of ours," Claris said. "We don't really have anything to do with him."

Claris had caught Straeger in a show or two, this in earlier days, in New York, long before Claris had any inkling that he would wind up in California, and so it had been something to get to know the performer and watch him close at hand. Straeger used to go bumbling along, light-hearted and devil-may-care, putting on a happy face, singing tunes to himself—"The Night Was Made for Love." He put on a happy face because he knew they couldn't stand you if you griped, if you were in the dumps and discontented. "She gives him fifty dollars a week spending money and he has to genuflect to her like she's a female Buddha," Claris had once heard him saying, the envy burning in him, speaking of an acquaintance, a member of the fraternity, who had already scored with a marriage. Claris had happened to be in a studio casting office when they were trying to fill some minor, unimportant part, and, on the impulse, thinking of Straeger as he had seen him on the stage in New York, had mentioned his name, getting the part for him—that was why Louis had the impression Straeger was represented by the agency and that Claris was associated with him. Straeger found out Claris had mentioned his name, and came to him, brimming and shy, genuinely pleased: "You did this for me—why?" Straeger, as soon as he had connected solidly with his lady, had had his teeth newly recapped, that expert theatrical job they did for the top stars, and Claris thought of the caps, the vacuum-fired procelain jacket crowns, strewn now somewhere on the concrete pavement of the highway; but what persisted most steadily in his mind as he gazed out at the hot, bright sunshine was the vision of Straeger's face, suddenly young and fresh, as he must have seemed when a boy, as he came forward that time and said, "You did this for me—why?"

CLARIS, ON LEAVING Louis, worked back to the public side of the hotel—the terrace, the lawns, the walks. He stood some distance away from the building, keeping close to a row of oleander bushes that lined the path. Everyone had gone in. It was the afternoon hiatus, the siesta. The grounds were empty; the terrace was heaped with chairs and tables. Down at the cottage, the hired chauffeur had the limousine ready for Hogue, and Claris knew the limousine had been parked there for the last forty minutes or so. A good many of the actresses liked to go shopping in the late-afternoon off hours, when the business was light and there weren't too many people around, and Claris supposed that Hogue— with the fears and constraints riding her—had most likely been stalling all day with this specific purpose in mind. But the constraints still had her fast; she still dallied and couldn't get herself out of the bungalow. Claris looked over to the hotel, to the different entrances from which Case might appear. Case should have been

coming out any minute now—he must have easily finished
changing and showering by this time—and Claris wished
the actress would bestir herself, that she would hurry
and get away. In the end they had to come to their senses.
Eventually, they shook out of their troubles and went
back to the studio—after all, the pictures always got
made. But if she collided with Case now, there would be
an uproar, a continuing diversion, something for her to
seize upon and brood on and busy herself with, and she
would be put that much further back on the road. It
suddenly began to worry Claris, as he wavered there in
the baking desert heat, that perhaps Case had gotten by
him in some way, that perhaps he was already inside the
cottage with her, battling with her. Claris didn't know.
Case could have come out by some other, hidden door.
He could have left earlier, while Claris was still talking
to Louis at the kitchen door, and in his uncertainty, rest-
less and perspiring, he decided to go down to the cottage, to look in on Hogue and see what was happening.

He started out, following the row of oleanders. He
went past the terrace and was moving on toward a
portico, toward an open flight of stairs they had there,
in back of the terrace, when he heard the quick, hasty
slidings of footsteps over the tiles, the sounds of some
kind of scuffle going on. It was the producer, Robert
Wigler, making a pass at a woman, attempting to fondle
her—in spite of the production standstill, in spite of his
crucial problems with the moneymen—and Claris had to
hold up, compelled to witness this incongruous encounter.

41

"Oh, for God's sakes, Wigler, amn't I in trouble enough?" the woman said. She was the one who had been having the hard time with her husband, the woman in the lobby. She was extremely attractive, as they all were, shapely and soft and tempting, but she wasn't as young as she looked, and she was suffering from arthritis. Her left shoulder and elbow were killing her. That was what she was doing on the portico stairs when Wigler fell on her—she had run out of aspirin and was going down for a new supply.

Wigler let her go. He stood back, his arms at his sides. Claris dug into the oleanders and waited. "You take your life in your hands the minute you walk out of the room," the woman said. She patted her hair in place, adjusted her dress, and walked on. Wigler turned around and plodded away.

Case wasn't with the actress. She was on the way out as Claris came into the cottage, but that didn't mean she was leaving immediately—Claris didn't know how long she had been on her way out. She wandered around the room, struggling to get herself in order so that she could leave. The rebelliousness and belligerence were gone. She was changed, worn down from the hours in the bungalow, from this unneeded shopping business with which she had saddled herself all day. Melanie waited at the door, bent on accompanying her mother to the stores, but Adele was too low in spirit, too spent, to resist the child or find fault with her. The thought of the chauffeur outside with the car weighed on the actress.

She had the chauffeur's feelings to consider now on top of her other distractions. She didn't want to go on holding the man up—"The next thing you know he'll spread it around I'm a nut," she said. But every time she started for the door, there was something to bring her back, something more to be done and delay her. Her scalp burned. She suddenly halted in her wanderings and held her hand to her head. This scalp-burning was a peculiar, mysterious ailment that always threw her into a depression. The burning came out in patches on her scalp. The sensation came and went. It was a neuritis, a misdirected neuralgia, a punishment sent down to plague her. In addition to her other vagaries and hallucinations, she thought she was being systematically persecuted. She hated comedians, was racked by old phantoms, believed that every time you turned a light out someone somewhere died. She was in a flutter. She couldn't control the fluttering. Claris knew it was no pose, no imaginary symptom to win her sympathy, or if it was, the discomfort to her was no less real. When she got busy, when she had some task to apply herself to, an appointment to meet, a breathlessness took hold of her. There was a racing, an agitation. Her heart palpitated. Sometimes she had a wild, unbelievably penetrating, wicked pain in her left arm, always the left arm, and during the fright of those moments, the only thing she could do was to hang motionless and hope and pray for the deep, bone-piercing pain to leave. She wouldn't talk to Claris. When he tried to say something to steady her, she just brushed past him and left him standing there. She didn't want to open herself up to him any more than she had to. She had exposed herself enough.

"You have to keep it to yourself. What should I do, bore people stiff with my miseries? You become anathema. They stay away from you in droves. The poor kids," she said, thinking of the twins, "the minute they see me, they run for the hills—you can't blame them." She understood how repugnant she made herself with her constant complaints, with her everlasting, self-centered concerns and excitements, and so her agony was doubled and re-doubled. She was worried about the twins. Out of some instinct or deviltry, the little boys made it a point to steer clear of her and the bungalow, and she hadn't seen them since early morning. She didn't know what they were doing, if they had had anything to eat. She hoped somebody was looking after them, that they wouldn't come to harm.

She finally got herself to the door. Claris thought it was over, that she would surely make it this time—she was halfway out of the door—but then, at the last minute, she turned back and flung herself into a new fit of despair. "Oh, look at me—just look at what I'm doing!" She was wearing that thin cotton wrapper they use when they're doing their hair, their makeup. Claris had wondered what she was doing, walking out of the bungalow in the wrapper. She had forgotten her dress. She had forgotten she was still in the wrapper. She had nothing on underneath but a slip, and this small mental lapse on her part upset and depressed her out of all proportion. "They'll take one look at me traipsing in with nothing on and they'll really think I'm crazy!"

She tore the wrapper off, went to one of the suitcases lying on the floor, stooped down and started rummaging for a dress she could wear. "Mother, everyone forgets," Melanie said, reasoning with her. "It's nothing, We all make absent-minded mistakes." And while Melanie coaxed and reasoned, while Adele kept bringing garments out of the suitcase, the door opened and Case was with them.

He had taken pains with his appearance, had shaved and smartened himself according to a certain style, and for an instant Claris glimpsed the image of the man as he once was, years back, light on his feet and resilient, like some Irish welterweight boxer just out of the barber shop, the world on a string; but the sparkle, the illusion, the whole witch-hazel air of well-being and style went glimmering before the violence of the reception Adele gave him. Claris didn't know where she had the energy in her. She drew herself up and came alive, a charge jolting through her body at the first sight of Case. It would have done no good if Claris had offered to leave, if he had tried to walk out. She wanted him there. She would have insisted on his presence—to defy Case, to show him she had allies, the agency behind her, and didn't need outsiders. "The sightseers and autograph-hunters have broken into the place," she said, almost glad, it seemed to Claris, to have Case in the room with her, almost eager to take him on even though she must have known she could only get hurt and come out second best in any tangle with him. Case ignored her. He stared at Claris, swiftly put him down for one of the college-educated nobodies they had on the staffs of the agencies, one of the family connections that had to be taken care of, and—so far as Claris could tell—paid him no further notice. "How are you, Melanie?" he said, forestalling Adele, keeping his back to her. He made conversation with the child—did she like it here? Was she having a good time? This was no place for her, he remarked, dry, looking around the room. No, she didn't mind it at the hotel, Melanie said, calm, steady, standing up for her mother. It was agreeable. It was quiet.

"What do you have to do here?" Case asked her.

"What do you have to do anywhere?" Melanie said. "And everything is air-conditioned."

Fannie came clattering in. She had evidently been on the lookout for Case too. She had no intention of letting her ex-husband rap into Adele unless she was on the spot to get between them. She waded in and started tidying up the room, grumbling—the twins had just been in the sprinklers, were sopping wet, needed a change from top to bottom, and were turning the hotel into a public playground. "What are you going to do now," she said to Case, "move mountains? Go ahead, convince her."

It always impressed Claris how these thugs, so wary and practical, so ready in their dealings to search through to the essential unworthiness of people, could, when it came to a woman, drop their guard and give themselves over with a complete, headlong abandon. Melanie trudged off into one of the bedrooms to find dry clothing for the twins, to get herself out of the way. Claris could hear her through the partition, puttering and pulling out drawers, while the contest went on between Case and her mother. It was a straight standoff affair, Case settling himself for the duration, acting as though it was foregone, open and shut, just a matter of time until she came to her senses and started back for the studio. He loomed above her, overbearing and peremptory, full of himself, so that it came as a shock to realize that he was actually short in stature, unprepossessing, squat. It was amazing how the pugnacity in him transformed him physically; without it he would be insignificant, would shrink back to size. This was their first meeting since she had returned from England. They hadn't seen each other for eighteen months, but the long separation didn't seem to trouble either one of them. They fell in stride, taking up apparently from where they had left off, and Claris, who was in there on a pass, so to speak, standing at the wall and overlooked, was able to get the inside flavor of their peculiar attachment, the way of them in the past, as they tugged and hauled and wouldn't leave each other alone. "He's got to have her," Fannie said from the sidelines, grinding at Case, not liking the way the tussle was going, seeing no good to it, no outcome, but helpless to stop it. "He has a pigeon to pick on and he can't hold himself in.

She don't want, so he wants. It's a must. The knocks he took from her, the insults, the rejections," Fannie said, working on the pillows on the couch, fluffing them up, wrenching the couch itself around into place. "If it was a man, he would throw him straight through the nearest window—there would be murder. But when it's Adele, everything is smiles."

"Did you drop in to feast your eyes?" Adele baited him. "Does it do your heart good to have the advantage over me, to see me right back where I started from?" She dressed him down. She might have known he'd be along. She could imagine how he saw himself—being the big man, spreading himself out.

"Famous lady," Case said. "International beauty." There had been all kinds of publicity—about the homecoming, the breakdown of her celebrated English marriage, the tantrums and irregularities with the picture now—and he wasn't going to let her smear herself up for good just to give the chiselers and column writers a field day. "When that ceiling turns to platinum," he said. He wasn't backing down. He wasn't taking no for an answer. He was still bitten by the freeway tieup; it griped him that he had had to beat out the traffic for three and a half hours. "You read this stuff they write about you in the papers and you think you have to live up to it. Watch out, you'll talk yourself into it and then you'll really be in trouble."

"You'd think he'd have some scruples and not go where he's not wanted, but he does, he does," Adele said.

Case had all the details on the production. He had taken a
hand, had moved in on the proceedings. He had made
it his business to see the backers or the potential backers,
and had given assurances that he would have her straightened out and would deliver her, and it infuriated her—
that he had made himself free with her, that he had given
people to think that he had authority over her. She com-
bated him with a blazing intensity, dancing on her feet
as she confronted him, half coming out of the slip, not
caring how it climbed up on her. "He walks in here like
the cat that swallowed the canary and starts issuing
pronouncements. Who gave you the right to speak for
me? Who made you the mastermind?"

"Leave it to her," Fannie said. "She knows what she's
doing, every time." Fannie meant the slip, the bare
shoulders and arms, the whole shuddering show of flesh.
Fannie thought it was a ploy, that Adele had consciously
or subconsciously contrived to be waiting for Case in
the slip in order to give him ideas and topple him.
"They're no dumbbells. They got it in them from the
day they're born—that's why they pay them fortunes.
Fool!" she said to Adele, defending her, taking her part,
at the same time slamming into her too. "If you didn't
want him, then why did you come here? You know you
did it for the express purpose of leading him on and giving him the needles, so what are you kicking about? You
got your wish—clap hands!"

Apparently there had been reconciliations or near-re-
conciliations, Claris gathered, times when Adele and Case

had gotten on, when they hadn't gotten on, when they had bickered and feuded and done who knew what things to each other—and the overlay of the past, of the stinging intimacies and self-betrayals, was more than she could keep out of her mind or bear. Case had the goods on her. That was the burn. That was why she sputtered and fizzled and fought him with such a vehement recklessness. In one way or the other he had been with her through the years. He knew her tricks, her foibles, the marriages and romances, the wonderful beginnings of them and then the bitter crash-landing endings; and in facing him, she had to face the messes and mistakes which were convulsing her and making it impossible now for her to work or breathe. To hit back at him, she taunted him on his own early failings. She threw it up to him how, when he first came to California, he had gone chasing to the class restaurants in town, to see and be seen with the movie elite. She rubbed it in—how in those days he used to sneak out to the big movie premières at the Carthay Circle Theatre, how he used to huddle in the crowd on the sidewalk, so that he could gawk and goggle at the stars. She threw it up to him that the management had once had to speak to him at the racetrack because he hopscotched over the boxes and socialized too much with the nabobs and celebrities. "Stupid, dumb broad," he said to her. "You know and I know and the lamppost knows sooner or later you're going to fold, so what are you raising an unnecessary holler for? Nobody expects you to be the great superstar

you think people think you have to be. Just go out there
and wiggle your butt, that's all they want from you. You
don't have to lose your nerve. You don't have to kill yourself. Just do what they tell you to do and you'll be all
right." He had her in his bones—the tops of stockings,
the pushed-up dress, the rolling on floors, on beds, the
whole irrational sexual phantasmagoria that grabbed and
goaded them. "Did I come anywhere near you?" he
reminded her. "You wanted me to stay away, so I stayed
away." He would have been perfectly happy to have nothing to do with her this time around, he said, but she was
pulling the roof down on her head and he had to step
in before it was too late. "Did I phone or try to contact
you in other ways, through second parties?"

But she had him there too. She was back at him like
a shot. He hadn't stayed away at all. He had had her
watched all the time. He had bribed people on the set,
the chief electrician, the unit manager, tipping them a
fifty apiece to bring back reports on her, and it was sur-
prising to see the sharp thrill of pleasure this tactical
victory gave her. "Do you think I didn't know? Did you
think I wouldn't find out?" She had had informants of
her own.

"Tell the truth, Harry," Fannie said, "isn't it embar-
rassing? Don't it go against the grain—to make yourself
small and spy on her?"

The fright went shooting through Claris. Of course—
that was how Case had known the exact details about the
scene on the set when Adele had made her speech to

the company and had crucified herself. Claris saw the danger he was in, the danger he had been running all along. He had assumed he was relatively safe— a flunky, one of the paid help that came and went around the actresses—but with Case hanging fast and bird-dogging her, Claris could see he was bound to be found out sooner or later. He thought back to the people on the set, the ones he knew and the ones who might know about him. He thought of Prescott, shooting his mouth off, spreading the good news around at the office and in all the other places too, Claris could bet, and he cursed himself for his laxness, for his chronic need to talk and let everyone know what he was doing.

Case was pounding hard. He had taken a good deal of punishment, was getting nowhere, and in the collision and infighting, in the sexual exacerbation, his patience was going fast. He was trying to get her to understand the position Wigler was in, to explain the nature of the financial arrangements. The banks supplied sixty or seventy percent of the financing, leaving it to the end-money investors to bring up the rest, to start the picture and to finish it, in this way guaranteeing the production. The end-money people were caught in a dilemma of their own. On the one hand, they were anxious to get in on a Hogue feature, her first since her return, a sure money-maker with all the to-do in the papers and the acclaim; but on the other hand, they were nervous about the delays. They were small folk, concerned about what they called the point of no return—that switchover when they were locked in and could only plunge on ahead. They were slow to put their signatures to a contract, and if they jumped and decided not to participate, there would be no bank loan, there would be no financing, Wigler would be left hung out to dry, with the considerable cash outlay already committed and spent, and the whole deal would collapse like a house of cards. Case was struggling to get this all in. "Bust Wigler, and I give you my word you'll never work again," he said, but she was too far gone, too swept up in her loathing and the remembrance of all that had gone on between them, to hear him out, to take time to worry about the financing, the end money and the point of no return.

"What you really want to do is have the say-so over me," she said. "That's why you walked in and tried to be the mastermind. You want to be the man in charge, telling everybody what to do."

"Would you be any the worse for it?" he said to her, lowering his voice, probably more in earnest than he knew. "Would it do you any harm, Adele, to have somebody in your corner to look out for your interests?"

"And then you'd be all over me like a ten-ton truck. That's what you're pushing for all the time. I'd be beholden to you. You'd like it. I'd be at your beck and call."

He let it all out. "Was it bad? At the time, did you suffer from it—the hyenas coming at you, the fights, the studio suspensions? Didn't it help to have a little muscle behind you when you needed it the most?" He went in close, bringing back old mortifications—the old unedifying, protracted bouts and sieges, the dependence on him, the ineptitude in her, the lack of will and courage. "Who are you? You got no strength, no stamina. Without the cameras, you wouldn't know what to do with yourself. You'd dry up and die. You'd wither away. The moves you made all your life," he went on, maddened and deadly, "going overboard for the first guy that comes along with a good line of bull—putting your faith in them, marrying them for good and forever, and then waking up four days later screaming you want out, your whole life is in ruins."

Fannie lunged at him. She wedged herself between them, beating him off. "What's the matter with you? What do you want from her?"

"Going down for the third time, hiding from people," Case said, walking away, annoyed with himself. He saw that he had said more than he had meant to say, that he had blown it and would have to come back to her at another time.

"Get him out of here," Adele said, trembling, sick.

"Knows just the right things to say to her, goes back to machine-gun tactics," Fannie said. "You see she's got the heebie-jeebies, she can't work, and you can only make it worse. What good did it do? Did you honestly think it would help?"

"She'll come off her high horse," Case said. "She just needs somebody to hate at the present time, so let her hate me. That's what I'm here for." The urgencies remained. He was thinking of the headaches, of the reporters now sifting in—he had seen some of them in the freeway tieup, stranded there along with everybody else, and he didn't know how the publicity would go and what it might do to the production. "Boy, she hates my guts. Her whole body started to shake the minute I walked into the room. I touched her hand, it was wet with sweat." He looked up, saw Claris there before him, remembered who he was, and felt obliged to make some sort of statement to him. "She'll come around," he said to Claris. Claris held still. "Everybody loses their self-confidence and goes into a slump now and then. You get your second wind, only she don't know that yet."

"Get him out of here," Adele said. She couldn't wait for him to leave. "So long as he's on the grounds of the hotel, I'm not budging. I don't need him to lay the law down and tell me the story of my life."

"Can't fall asleep unless the light is shining straight into her eyes and the radio is going full blast," Fannie said to her, still overheated and angry. "What did you think was going to happen? You knew he was no Albert Schweitzer. You knew what you would get. Love's sweet song," she said, advancing on Case, starting him to the door. "The gifts he showered on her, the attentions, the jewelry from Brock's—gone with the wind, water under the bridge."

"Why do you take care of the twins and do everything for her?" Case said, carping with her now over the neglect, the children living out of suitcases and everything let go.

"What should I do, throw her out?"

"If you didn't watch out for the twins, then she would have to do it herself and it would give her a sense of responsibility. Too broken down even to get a nursemaid for the kids," Case said, but Fannie had him arguing at the door, was holding it open, nudged and pushed, and they were gone.

————→MELANIE CAME OUT of the bedroom, carrying a pile of clothing—underwear, sweaters. She obviously had not wanted to leave while Case was still in the room, while the dust-up was in progress, and it was clear she was reluctant to leave the bungalow even now. But the evening desert chill was coming on, and she had to get the twins into dry clothes; she had to see to it that they had their dinner. She trundled past Claris, hiding whatever she was feeling behind the thick glasses, as she customarily did, keeping steady, acting as though everything was in order, normal, and went out the door. Claris was left alone with the actress. She didn't keep it to herself this time. She spoke out without reserve, using him, trusting him, not trusting him. She knew there was nothing much she could expect from him. She had been around, was under no illusions, knew exactly what she had in this fast pickup shuffle in the sack with him, but in the mood she was in she didn't care what she said or who heard it. She had to have someone. She was on the skids, as far back as they could get, tied in knots, blocked, tortured by the passing of the years. "How fast they come out with the once-over—'She still looks good.' It's the battle cry around here. You hear it all over," she said, harsh and unhappy. She had little children to take care of, was unable to sleep, was ridden with hypochondria, with the mass of her neuroses and afflictions, the scalp-burning and palpitations—and yet she had this fierce, perverse streak in her to resist with all her strength and stand them all off. "You want things from people. You make demands," she said. "You hold bitter grudges in your mind and brood because you think they're running out on you and are false and ungrateful— when all the time of course the truth is they're up to their ears in troubles themselves and probably have their own private grudges, thinking people are letting them down and are self-seeking and rotten. So you don't know what you're doing. You hit out and screw everything up, and then you not only have your original miseries still to contend with but you've antagonized everyone who might come near you in the bargain." Claris supposed this was her way of chopping up on herself because she had come this far along and had no friends, no group to belong to; or else it was a backhanded slap at him, letting him know that she was reduced to people like him, people who worked for her.

It had been a sore point between them, a recurring irritation, although they had never spoken of it, that he had had to go slogging off in the evenings, that he had a wife there, a home. Fortunately his wife was away now, so he had room to move around in and could give the actress all the time she wanted, and he told her he was staying at the hotel, that he wasn't driving back, although he didn't think he needed to mention the reason to her. "What's the use of burning yourself up?" he said to her. "What difference does it make what Case has to say to you or what you have to say to him? You're only getting in a state over him because it's easier to do that than buckle down to the work." But she waved him off and made him stop.

"I know I'm not making sense. I don't have to have you to tell me I'm being illogical."

The hired chauffeur had long ago left; Fannie must have sent him away, or the chauffeur must have realized the time was passing and that the trip into town was off. They had the cottage all to themselves. Claris had heard of cases of other performers who had their problems and went through a similar commotion, but he had never witnessed the phenomenon at first hand. He couldn't understand the stark, fanatical violence of their feelings and he didn't know if this violence was assumed, exaggerated, or whether there was some special validity to it. He wouldn't have known how to deal with these other performers and he didn't know what to do with Adele now. She sat in the chair, not looking at him, lost in herself. She felt as though her teeth ached, she said. It reminded her, she said, of a time, years back, when she was a girl, when she had seared the roof of her mouth on a pizza pie. "You know, the melted cheese, it sticks, it clings," she started to explain and then languished and quit explaining. She was red-headed, or what was known as strawberry blond, more reddish than blond, with the thin, clear skin and coloring that went with her hair; Claris could see the freckles still on her face—and the freckles, the high, insistent coloring, together with the dark shooting splotches of her eyes, gave a jarring urgency to the charge of her protest. She sat loosely in the slip, regarding the body in the slip with a kind of angry, detached impatience—the body perpetually pummeled, massaged, costumed, rigged out, and displayed. She had had operations, a hysterectomy, and she spoke up against the hysterectomy too, against the glib, inside trade term the movie doctors used among themselves in connection with the surgical procedure—the Joe E. Brown, the doctors called it, because of the wide line of the abdominal incision. Nothing about her gave her peace; she had reached that point where, if it had anything to do with her, she was at once displeased and wearied. She railed at the dieting and reducing she had to do. She had fits of nibbling, could eat the whole day through, she said. "Putting it on, hacking it off—suddenly you swell out like a balloon," she said. Claris supposed it was this persistence, this force of will, the sheer wanting and refusal to subside, that accounted for the difference in them, that caused certain actresses to project, as the saying was, and come across and draw the attention from the audience. He was disconcerted by the living fact of the person here.

He was alarmed by the clamor in her, by the shameless, uncontrolled outpouring, and, in the awkwardness of the moment, worrying about the actress and taken up with her, he juggled his own fears. He saw the hopelessness of the position he was in, and he wondered what he thought he was doing, standing by idly, waiting on the actress—waiting for what, he asked himself.

She had gone back in her mind to Harry Case. She was talking about an incident that had occurred in his office—this was a number of years ago, when the Las Vegas strip was first going up, when they were starting to build the row of gambling hotels. Case had taken a spread of fancy offices in Los Angeles, mainly for the sake of the movie crowd whom he followed so ardently in those days and wanted to impress and be part of. She had gone up to see the place, and she told now—whether to demean Case or score him off, for whatever good it did her—how he had gone after her in the office, bawdy and abashed, still sitting in the desk swivel chair, wriggling after her in the chair, on its casters, pressing her into the corner with his knees. She told of another occasion, when Case had come calling on her at her house, when she had still been in the bedroom, dressing. The maid had told him he would have to wait, but he had pushed past the maid, gone to the bedroom, and poked his head inside the door. "You've got a nerve, walking in here," she had begun, but then he had dangled the present he had brought her, diamond earclips from Brock's, and she had invited him in—to the lacy stuff, the garter straps, the high-heeled

mules, the whole undressed business they yammered for.
"What a fool I was," she said, speaking to Claris, remembering. " 'Come in! Come in!' I told him." She
wasn't scoring off Case or running herself down; what
she was really doing was trying to get back the feeling
of those days—the assurance, the easy spirits. She was
still fighting, holding on, talking to herself, striving for
that morning when you wake up and everything is mirac-
ulously lifted, the depression vanished, and you go speeding off again. She talked of old escapades, times when she
had eluded Case and infuriated him, when she had gone
stealing off with a weekend companion, some good-
looking leading man from the studio, her partner as rash
and eager for the spree as she was. She was a star, immediately recognizable wherever they might go, so they
had this extra hazard to play with and counter—they
had had to seek out obscure desert resorts, Soboba Hot
Springs, Murrieta, places at that time still off the beaten
path and remote. She spoke of the little old Jews, blink-
ing in the sun and musing, who clustered at those out of
the way hotels for the mineral baths, for their health.
She told how, sitting on the passenger's side of the car,
she had had to duck her head down at the dashboard
when they came driving up to some bellboys or young
people who would have known who she was. And as she
brought out these remembrances, confidences which she
would no doubt later on regret and reproach herself for,
as Claris listened in the unnatural, enforced intimacy, he
saw how it had once been for her. He sensed the excite-

ment that had possessed and sustained her and that she was now trying to recall—the excitement of those forbidden afternoons on the desert, the excitement of her partner's excitement.

"When you're young, when it's all going for you, you just get out on the set, and whatever they want you to do, you just rip it off. You don't know what it is when you have it, when it all comes easy. You do the scene without thinking about it. You don't have to think. It's all in the way you feel. It's the feeling in you. I am a clown," she said, still unyielding, trying to make him understand why it had been once possible for her and why it was no longer so. "It's like when you go some place and you sit in your hat and gloves and you suddenly don't know where you are or what's happening around you or even that you exist."

$\mathbf{F}$ANNIE HAD HER office just off the reception desk in the lobby, and the people connected with the production used the area around the office as a sort of unofficial meeting place, gravitating there for news, for developments, or simply to keep in touch with one another in the emergency. It was odd how Claris had become fully oriented to the place, the paths, the general layout, the location of the different halls and exits all at once becoming familiar to him, as they do, say, when we are suddenly summoned to a hospital and have to live through a period of crisis. He had spent the night at the hotel—it had been no problem for Louis to send out for a shirt for him, to fix him up with the toilet articles he needed. The steward was prepared for such things and was more than happy to be of service. Claris was due at the bungalow. He knew he was more or less expected to turn up and spend time with Adele, and he intended to be with her eventually, but he lingered on, out of inertia or indecision, to see what was happening. He was coming in off the grounds to have another look at the lobby when Wigler, also wandering about, aimless and neglected, picked him off. They had fallen in with each other on and off all morning—it was part of Claris's job to make himself available to the producer—and so they kept up the vigil in company again, Claris again required to listen to the older man's dry, urbane homilies.

The paths were empty; the terrace with its clutter of tables and chairs lay deserted; everyone had gone indoors to escape the sun. It was the siesta. The married couple, the one engaged the day before in the heated dispute in the lobby, had made up their differences. Claris and Wigler had seen them together on the terrace earlier in the day, the husband smooth-shaven and replenished, all trace of anguish mysteriously disappeared, as if it had never existed. The wife had quieted him, in the ways they had; and now, as the long afternoon siesta began, as Claris and Wigler came up to the portico—the portico with the open staircase, where the married couple had their room—they inadvertently heard the woman's voice, infinitely serene and kind, softly reprimanding, "Oh, you are naughty." The woman's voice, the wayward fragment, in the sunny stillness, had an effect on Wigler.

"They're all secret agents," he murmured to Claris, as they moved along, as they headed on to the office. "Well, it's a lot of fun," he said, distracted, with his broad understanding. "You think it's nothing, to put your hand under a woman's dress?"

He himself had been unlucky straight down the line with women, he said; he didn't have the knack. He had

a spoiled marriage behind him, had been through all
kinds of vicissitudes, had once attempted suicide—Claris
believed he had once seen something about it in the
papers—and the woman's tenderness, coming at this time
when everything was tense and precarious for him, set
him off, leading him to reveries which ordinarily, no
doubt, he would have held back from his closest friends,
but which—under the circumstances, drifting and idling,
groping for something to say—he didn't mind sharing
with Claris, an almost total stranger to him. He used to
live at the beach, he said. They had had a house, he and
his wife—he was talking about his marriage, its dissolution and how it had come to pass. "Up the coast, Malibu,
past Malibu, farther, not far from Point Mugu, Port
Hueneme—you know, the naval stations. There were
these exceptionally big grocery bills," he continued,
going to the heart of his account, "and not that I wanted
to be picayune about it, you understand, but it was genuinely puzzling to me—after all, we were just two people,
my wife and me. So I looked into it, out of curiosity.
Well, it's a peculiar thing, but it so happens that I have
never been a beer drinker. I don't care for it, and the big
grocery bills—they were for beer. The sailors, the sailors,"
he said, looking away. It was this entirely accidental
curiosity about the grocery bills that had awakened him,
that had opened up a whole Pandora's box of revelations.
He told Claris all about the attempted suicide, speaking
freely. The strain was getting to Wigler. He carried
himself with a certain presence, with the courtly au-

thority and calm of the seasoned producer, and bore his losses bravely, but the truth was he was actually without resources in the emergency. For him there was no point of no return. He had long ago gone past it. "All my life, I signed my name to papers which, even while I was signing them, nobody in their right mind would ever dream they would actually be able to hold me to account," he had said to Claris in an earlier, equally wry, offhand admission. He had signed notes, had mortgaged his house, had given guarantees which he couldn't possibly fulfill, and everything for him hinged on the actress. That was why he treated her with such fearful delicacy and wouldn't go near the bungalow. That was why he flitted about in the background. The attempted suicide had occurred in a moment of deep dejection, in a disgraceful, deluded fit of self-pity, he said to Claris. He had checked into a motel, swallowed the handful of sleeping tablets. "The whole schmear, stretched out on the bed, waiting for the end, then seized with panic, calling the Fire Department—'Hurry up, send the ambulance, pump me out!'"

They had reached the office. Some people from the studio had driven out and were waiting for Wigler— the unit manager, office personnel, bringing in the daily cost sheets and other reports that had to be signed.

"I don't know," Wigler said, vacant, musing, staring at his assistants. He couldn't carry a tune, he said. He couldn't whistle and it somehow worried him. "That is, I have it in my head, the song, but when I try to get it out, when I want to sing it—I can't." He couldn't seem to daydream any more, and this, too disturbed him. This business of being unable to daydream had something to do with television, he thought. You could daydream with the radio on, but not with television—watching the tube took up too much of the mind, didn't leave room for day-dreaming. He walked away.

Harry Case was inside the office with Fannie. The door was left standing open, and Claris could see them close together, communing, waiting, Fannie busy with her work at the desk while Case sat alongside in the visitor's chair.

"What are you so sore about?" Fannie said to him.

"Ah, that she makes such an obvious mark of herself, always the fall guy."

"Hello. He first wakes up. What else is new?"

Their voices were subdued; they had settled down with each other. They were aware Claris was loitering in the hall outside the door, but they were used to the sight of him, considered him as part of the family, and went on conversing. Case was talking about the bustup of his big romance with Adele, about the first parting of the ways—in the lull, passing the time, he was letting his thoughts run backwards. As Claris got it, from what Case was saying, there had been a proposal of marriage; Adele at the last minute had reneged, had wept and begged off; and, apparently, from that point on nothing had ever been the same again. Case was going back over the years, to the events that had finished off his marriage and brought on the divorce, and it struck Claris, as he listened on—this man, so battle-hardened, fighting the bloat and the passage of time, dwelling now on the past, while his ex-wife worked away on her bookkeeping at the desk alongside and heard it all without a flicker. Claris had a mental picture of Adele in those days, on the loose, going with gangsters, or people she thought were gangsters, for the thrill, and then getting scared and scurrying for cover as the situation turned serious on her and became too much to handle.

"Boy, she cried—she cried her eyes out," Case said. "She knew right then and there she was making the mistake of a lifetime. 'Don't cry,' I told her. 'I'm going, I'm going.'"

"You hung one on her," Fannie said. "She told you to take a walk, and you came out the hero."

Case wasn't concerned about the producer. He knew Wigler had no choice—Wigler could go only with Adele and he would hang on, scramble, stall, and do everything he could to keep the project afloat. Case was counting on Adele to exhaust herself. He expected her to get fed up, to act on impulse again and pack and go back and get through with it—that was why he was now staying clear of the bungalow, to give her time to reflect. In the end, when you got right down to it, after all the tantrums and temperament, you went where the money told you to go, he said, and she was strapped. Case, who had taken it on himself to know everything about the actress, evidently knew all about the state of her finances, too. It

was a long time between pictures for her. She had to
work. Case and Fannie both were keeping an eye on the
hired chauffeur. The driver would be the tip-off—they
apparently had an arrangement with him, Claris gathered, to let them know as soon as Adele made her move.
"What'll she do with herself in the bungalow all day?
Who has she got to talk to—the kid, Melanie? She'll get
bored," Case said, thinking aloud, and Claris, standing at
the door, felt the flush go through him. He saw the place
he had in the setup. He saw what Adele wanted him
around for, to be on hand and divert her, while she went
on with her antics and kept them all in a ferment.

"What does she want?" Case said.

"What she wants—she wants the moon," Fannie said.
"She remembers when she was the belle of the ball, the
center of all eyes. She was four times box-office champion
—you got an idea what that does to a person? It's the
breath of life to them. It gives them confidence and moral
support. They feel they're anointed and can do no wrong,
and when it blows over, naturally it's a shock and they go
to pieces and can't stand themselves. You can understand
it. She wants everything to be the way it used to be."

"When she went running up to the balcony between
shows at the Paramount and necked?" Case said, slant-
ing the shot in. The studios used to send the young stars
out to the big movie houses on personal appearances in
those days; Claris knew the story—how Adele had gone
up to the balcony between her stage appearances, during
the matinees, to look at the feature in the dark with a

70

companion, to cuddle. Case was waiting for the actress to get tired of her shenanigans and go back to the studio, but the afternoon lengthened and there was no sign of movement at the bungalow. The driver didn't send word, and so Case's voice grew testy and impatient, and he slanted the digs in. "When she went sporting weekends with the boys to Soboba Hot Springs and Carlsbad?"

"Yes," Fannie said. "Yes." She stood up at the desk and started stowing the ledgers away. "A lot she knows what she's doing. She comes out of nothing, her mother working there in the beauty shop on Highland Avenue, the two of them fighting over the one good dress, eating out of cans, eating hamburgers. They found her in the malt shop, playing hookey—for God's sakes, she was still going to high school." Fannie was talking about the beginning. The casting people had needed a young sexy girl to be assaulted, to get the picture's story off. They had walked Adele in front of the cameras for four or five hundred feet of film—that was all it had been; she hadn't even had a line—and the walk, the four hundred feet of film had been enough. "They put her in a tight skirt and boom, the people started throwing themselves on the floor—overnight she was a star. 'Fannie, I got to have a husband,' she told me, thunder and lightning, when I pleaded with her, when I tried to talk her out of marrying the piano player that time, the one who later went nuts and wound up at Camarillo. And what about the Army flyer, the colonel? Two weeks after the wedding, she had to meet him in Pittsburgh and she went right past him in the lobby of the hotel without recognizing him—she didn't even know who he was."

"They'll marry anyone," Case said.

Claris felt he ought to be getting away from the door—he had been standing at the one spot long enough. The floor of the lobby lay cool in the dimness. Wigler was still talking to his people a short distance up the hall. They made a group. And Claris, as he started to step away from the office door, glancing over in the direction of Wigler's group as he did so, saw, or for an instant thought he saw, Dick Prescott, his associate at the agency. But it wasn't Prescott. It was a production employee who resembled him to an extent. But just then—as so oftens happens in these cases for no reason we can ascertain—seconds after Claris mistakenly believed he had seen Prescott and after he realized it wasn't Prescott, Prescott himself came bounding into view, swinging along to Wigler and his group, and joining them. Claris was joggled off balance by this coincidence, by this seeming double vision, and he was also ruffled by the jaunty manner of Prescott, bouncing on his feet and hustling along as he did—when he turned and found Harry Case confronting him. Fannie in the meanwhile had left the office to go off on some other duty, and Case, with time on his hands, had come by to chat. Case tested him, pried, tried to draw him out. It was an uneasy, jittery interview, innocently enough meant by Case but peculiarly taxing for Claris. Case saw Claris as a person in another class—college-educated, new-style, with a good twenty years or more on him. Case had probably been told about Claris's wife, a wealthy girl, non-pro, not in the arena—someone invariably brought up the subject of Claris's marriage; it was his great claim to distinction —and this stratum, so far removed from Case's experience and novel to him, intrigued or amused him, so he probed now, with all his practicality and down-to-earth thug's realism, thinking maybe they had the answers, maybe these folks knew a way. He asked Claris questions about his job—did he like it, did it keep him busy? It was different from his time, Case commented, running liquor and selling it, bootlegging, back in the old Prohibition days. He purposefully steered the conversation around to the circle of Claris's friends, sincerely interested in getting some notion of how it was with them, how they acted and thought. "You talk to people today that were *born* in nineteen hundred forty and something. They don't even remember Prohibition. Listen, these new chicks nowadays—these young kids padding barefoot in the unit apartments, preparing dinner for their hubbies, humming the hit tunes from the big Broadway shows—are they on the con?" he asked Claris. "Do they work their hubbies for dough to give to their families? Do they cheat?"

Claris kept wooden. He stood up to Case, demurring, saying enough to get by, as Case went on with this gritty, idle third-degree, Case sleepy-eyed and sly, no doubt spreading himself out a little for Claris's benefit, letting him see a mellower, unsuspected side to his nature, it never once entering his head that Claris all the while was carrying on a business with the actress. Case wrote him off as some lightweight laid away in a sinecure cooked up for him by his in-laws, laid away in a cushy marriage he wasn't going to do anything to upset. Claris felt a spasm of anger at Prescott, his colleague. He knew exactly what Prescott was up to—putting in a five-minute appearance at the hotel-resort so that he would be covered, so that he could truthfully tell the bosses at the agency, Skip Meyerson, Herbie Cottrell, that he had been on the grounds every day. Claris was surprised that Prescott had driven the hundred miles to show up at the hotel at all. He knew Prescott had long ago shunted the whole responsibility over to him, telling Meyerson and Cottrell the inside scoop, giving them the full, juicy details, and Claris bitterly wondered how long it would take for the word to go traveling around until it got to Case.

There was a harsh, abrupt flurry of movement up the lobby. Wigler had been going over the daily budget sheets with his assistants, checking the production costs as they accrued each scheduled day. These statements, which the assistants brought out for him to sign and for which he was personally liable, were the official forms that were to be filed with the auditors, and the figures, in black and white, had taken a certain toll. It was—as was soon evident—a remark from Prescott which provided the final abrasion and set off the outburst. But essentially, at bottom, what provoked Wigler, what was responsible for the breakdown, was the lowness of spirit, the waiting and seepage, the constant aura of misfortune that clung to him. Claris looked up at the first harsh shifting sounds. The cluster around Wigler appeared to be opening up, the men retreating as if on a signal. Wigler's voice was heard speaking to Prescott. "Don't go off! What is this going off! What is so much more important elsewhere that you must go off to attend to it?" And then it broke—inchoate, crazed. It was an astonishing exhibition. "All right, so it's a joke—I am over the barrel and can do nothing. But what is the joke, what will the celebration be if the backers go out on me, the banks to follow, and I am faced with catastrophe?" His eyes were shut tight. The stout body, hitherto so rigorously poised, so stately, heaved up and down with a sickening abandon. It all spilled out—the disappointments, the production delays, the broken marriage, and the six-packs of beer. "What am I here, goddammit, a booby, that I should be fobbed off with second-class help and office boys? What am I, a clod to be ridiculed and tortured to death? I want service! I want Skip Meyerson! I want top priority!" He was booming. The panic rode him. He had given way. He was terrified by the specter of the end-money investors, by their cold-blooded aloofness and iron will, by the remorseless ever-building publicity—through it all, the newspaper reporters had been sending in their bulletins; the wire services had come on and were now adding their mite to the sensation. In the grip of his hysteria, Wigler saw the debacle with a great white blinding clarity.

"You will see, I will be forced to suspend, the project will go to hell, and we will all watch the money running straight down the sewer!"

Case went up the hall, moving like a prize fighter. He took hold of the producer, steadied him, kept talking to him. The paroxysm was halted; and while Case was still busying himself with Wigler, while the others looked on and Claris knew he wouldn't be noticed, he backed off and slipped out of the lobby, leaving by the main entrance—he had spotted Prescott, at the height of the confusion, ducking out through a side door, as he would, and Claris wanted to intercept him before he got to the parking lot and disappeared.

Prescott had a girl stashed away. She was waiting in the car—that was the reason he had driven out to the resort, to use the trip as an excuse to get clear of the office and make a day of it. He had put in his time, had shown himself on the scene, and now was on the run, nothing on his mind but the girl and the workout ahead of him, and so it was a jolt, a rupture in the mood, when Claris caught up with him in the parking lot and started talking to him about the problems with the actress. Prescott had a thief's brain, with a thief's ready-made collection of guidelines and maxims. "That's right, why should I jeopardize myself?" he had told Claris the morning before, flat, without a quiver, when he had turned the whole mess over and had gone skipping off. "If the man says he didn't say it, then the man says he didn't say it," Prescott would say, smug and shiny, to the man's face—this when there was some question over the facts in the case, when Prescott already had the advantage over the fellow. Claris remembered they had once been in a tight spot with a client—they had given their word to the actor on some matter, had then found out they couldn't keep it, and Claris had wondered what they could do. "No contest. I'll tell him we didn't tell him. I'll tell him we lied," Prescott had said, pat, solving the dilemma. Claris knew you had to be grateful to people like Prescott in this world because you never had to feel sorry for them. But it was a different story when you had to go to them and deal with them. Claris pressed hard. The time was going; it was all closing in. Wigler had blown, asking for the head men, and the least Claris and Prescott could do to appease him was to make sure they were both of them there. Claris explained what he was up against, that Hogue was around the bend, that he had no influence on her.

"I know, laddie, sure. Listen. Let me think about it. Let me see what I can do. I'll get back to you."

"You don't understand," Claris said. "I'm not discussing it with you or asking for your opinion. I'm telling you straight out—I want you on the place. Don't you see, with you around, I won't be so exposed." Claris didn't want to be isolated. They all knew he meant nothing at the agency. They would soon start getting suspicious, asking themselves how it happened that he alone was left with the actress, asking themselves what he was doing there. Claris didn't want any of them asking questions about him. "You know my situation," he said to Prescott. "I can't take a rap. I need a hand. With the two of us here together, I can still work out of it and not get hurt."

"Listen," Prescott said, "let's not make a pest out of ourself. I told you I'd think about—."

"I'll slam you!" It went shooting out of him. He was ready to tear into Prescott. "You son of a bitch! You're not fading out and laying it all on me. You're getting paid. This is your job too!"

"You don't own me. I don't have to take it from you," Prescott said, startled, the breath out of him. His voice broke. He reasoned with Claris, wheedling, placating. "What do you want, to have it on a platter? You got no complaint with me. If you want to take her, then go ahead, all right. You got qualifications, the athletic prestige—you can make it. But why should I do the work for you? Where do I come in?" Claris stared at him. The anger ran out of him. He saw what Prescott meant. There were people who cashed in on actresses. Claris could think immediately of three or four names—men who had latched on, marrying them or living with them, who had set themselves up as producers, as figures to be reckoned with. If you controlled a top motion-picture personality, you counted, you could be solidly established—and Claris didn't know if that had been the plan, if he had been on the make all the while, or what it was exactly that had been in his head when he had gone after the actress and taken up with her. He saw the loose skin on Prescott's face, the crud fear sweating out.

"What did you have to make me look bad in front of the broad for?" Prescott said. "You can't have it both ways. If you want to make it, then you have to work for it. They're not giving anything away for nothing."

He hurried over to the car, to his date there, wrenched and harassed, the chesty arrogance shaken out of him for once, the edge of his afternoon's pleasure rubbed off and tarnished.

━━━━━➤ FOR ALL CLARIS KNEW, Wigler
was already raising a row with the agency toppers, starting in motion there was no telling what inquiries and
rumors; Case was waiting nearby to hear from the hired
chauffeur, expecting the inactivity and tedium to pall
on Adele; and Claris, aware of the risks to himself, that
he was crossing Case and playing it fine, nevertheless
went ahead with the actress. He had her in Louis's room,
using the steward's quarters over the kitchen as a hiding
place where they could be by themselves for an hour
or two. There was a small delivery area behind the
kitchen for the supply trucks, well away from the public
side of the hotel, the area circling around the dusty, be-
grimed pepper tree they usually had in those places. "You
could drive to the door," Louis had said in his clipped,
reserved undertones when he had willingly put the room at
Claris's disposal, if Claris wanted it, such as it was, he
had said; when they had set it up between them before-

hand, in the way these things were done. Two or three cars were generally parked in the delivery area, and Louis had said there was no reason why Claris's car would be noticed among them. "Leave the key. I'll take it down to the parking lot and then get it back to you later," Louis had quietly assured him, promising his help, that all would go well. So, while the siesta was still on, Claris had driven her in broad daylight to the kitchen area. They had silently filed into the doorway and gone up the flight of wooden stairs together, hoping they wouldn't run into anyone, trusting it all to the luck of the moment—that brazen chance-taking that was part of the character of these outings. The room was makeshift —the bare boards of the floor showing, the sun coming through the worn, yellowed window shades. Claris stood back and had to wonder at the self-possession of the actress. The battered room didn't faze her. She made herself at home, not minding the bare boards, the old iron bed, the torpor in the room. Claris wasn't sure the squalor of the place didn't in some way give her an added gust of gratification. When they had been together on those other sessions, when he had gone up to see her, ostensibly to talk her into coming down to the set and the cameras, they had used her dressing-room suite for the purpose— those bleached, uninhabited, sunbaked furnished apartments the studio had on the lot for the convenience of the stars; outside, on those occasions, while the time went by, the life of the studio rumbled on around them—and Claris now had the same guilty feeling of seclusion, of secret wrong-doing, which he supposed was also part of the package, the lubricity and lure.

The room had an L-shaped extension or alcove at one end. Adele was busying herself in this cubbyhole, combing her hair and undressing. She naturally assumed she was out of view for the moment, and she would have been except for the mirror on the wall. From where Claris was standing, at the bed, he had a straight line of vision to her reflection, and so for a time, while she stirred and stooped, wrapped up in her private rancors and resolves, whatever they were, not thinking she was being observed, he held still and watched her in this odd, surreptitious way. He saw her face, fleeting and stern in the mirror, the face which gave her trouble, which she couldn't relate to herself and found alien or unfamiliar, which she said didn't go with her. He had been in binds before, of his own doing, binds which it seemed he had almost deliberately sought out; but he had never had this foreboding, this sense of guilt. He wasn't proud of himself, lurking in the pocket, an interloper, a ringer, quailing with fear at every turn that he would be pulled out in the open and smashed. He honestly didn't know why he was abetting her—whether it was venery, whether he was looking to break his head and get smashed, whether it was for the advantage he might reap by associating himself with her, whether it was to help her, because he had gotten involved with her and couldn't run out and forsake her, whether it was the plain, unmitigated fool

in him. "Harry isn't going to like you for this," she had
said to him in a sidelong japery as they had gone up
the flight of stairs together toward the steward's room.
When Claris had been with her in the bungalow, in the
interval just before he had brought her here, she had
spoken of the peculiar giddiness, that extreme, grotesque
excitation or delirium that sometimes overtook and un-
hinged a performer in the pitch of the work. Claris knew
what she meant. He had seen it now and then—the performer overtaxed, teetering and bathed in sweat, all fired
up, the eyes wild and strained. It came from panic, from
the rank dread of failure and humiliation; and as Claris
held motionless now during this brittle business with the
mirror, the misgivings and uncertainties working in him,
he had an understanding of how it had been for her. It
wasn't just the tight skirt, the fluke of her sudden discovery and overnight success, when they took her out of
high school and the malt shop. Being discovered and
breaking in wasn't all there was to it. The success had to
be constantly nailed down, renewed. She had had it in
her to apply herself. She had known what was required,
and Claris visualized her in the years gone by, fighting
with such resources as she had to fight with, fearing
it wouldn't last, going up against men whose full-time
occupation it was to maneuver and bargain, yearning for
a mentor, an adviser, who could guide her into the right
moves and be her friend.

"You feel all lit up like a Christmas tree," she had
said in the bungalow, speaking of the delirium. "Your

eyes feel like neon lights. Under the strain and excitement, you don't know what you're liable to say or do.
You could come out with anything. If somebody came
by and put a finger on you, you could go shooting straight
through the ceiling."

Working at the agency and around the different
studios, Claris had seen glimpses of certain actors and
actresses who were similarly infected with this doubt and
inner panic. He thought of one man in particular, a top
star, among the first ten, who at the same time was shaky
and unfit, close to the borderline or over it. They didn't
know what they had, what it was in them that accounted
for their great good fortune. They didn't know how to
present it, manipulate it, embellish it, portion it out—since
they didn't know what it was or whether in fact they had
anything at all. "Star quality," the executives in the front
offices called it, using this term as a definition, a term
which of course didn't explain anything. So-and-so had it;
if the picture went badly at the box office, then he didn't
have it, had had it, had lost it—it was gone. "Who? How
can you say that? Is that so? You don't say!" the man
Claris was thinking of would say, registering an engag-
ing humility, an entreating helplessness, in response to
almost any chance remark. He was hamming it, putting on an act. That was his act. They adopted guises,
sometimes using a set of them interchangeably, understanding it was a guise, that they were hamming it and
putting up a front—but not knowing any other way of
getting by, not knowing what was expected of them

or what they were supposed to have. Sometimes the front collapsed on them. They would dispense with impersonations and mimicry, would come out in their true selves, what there was to their true selves, and then there would be shattering scenes of violence. Claris had heard stories of the most outlandish excesses, savage bouts of self-destructiveness, breakdowns, scandals. The mind became jumbled, turned in on itself, balked; became vacuous, spent. Adele herself was hung up on some theory which she had evolved on her own. She believed her special effectiveness with the audience was spontaneous, something organic, beyond control. She believed it was the product of the nervous system you were endowed with, and she was convinced her nerves were used up, that you were given just so much. That was why she fretted over the vertical ridges on her fingernails and took to heart the smatterings she read in the medical columns in the morning newspaper—she thought her nerve fibers lay wasted and shriveled and squiggly in their grooves there in the tissue, and were failing her.

"It's a funny thing, no matter how far gone you are, you always know what you're doing," she had commented to Claris in the bungalow, just before they had left for the steward's room. She was thinking of past performances, of previous alarms and crises in which she had figured. "There's always something inside of you, watching you—you know perfectly well you're being impossible and making outrageous demands. But you don't stop. You just go right ahead. You do it." She had delivered

the words with a perverse, almost vindictive relish—she
clearly realized the size of the difficulties she was causing
and that she was behaving badly and would most likely
regret it, and yet she was ruthlessly determined to carry
through. Claris hadn't tried to argue with her or sway her
in the bungalow. He was conscious of the unsavory, impersonal nature of their relationship—that it was all
accident, that he was an expedient, that they had fallen
in together only because he was the agent and happened
to be there and because she was marooned and had no
one else. She had pushed behind her the hallucinations,
the scalp-burning, the neuroses and palpitations. She no
longer let herself be ridden with mortifications. "The
biddies with their high couture and dead behinds," she
had said contemptuously, referring to the stylish women
guests at the hotel, to the expensive, well-fitting girdles
they wore. She didn't care what the stylish ladies thought,
those second and third wives who had it made and whose
hazy, indolent calm she noted so bitterly and wished
she could emulate. "They probably go around saying how
I ought to be willing to do anything to find a niche for
myself and that my whole life is coming apart." Claris
had told her something of what was taking place down at
Fannie's office in the lobby, and his report filled her with
a senseless, disproportionate spread of elation. She
gloated. She forgot about the women guests. She saw
that she had the upper hand, that they all had to come
to her and dance to her tune, that without her there
was no picture, and it sent a rush of hope and exultation

through her, although Claris couldn't imagine what she was hoping for or thought she could win with her crazy show of defiance. "They're frightened to death of the hullabaloo," she had chortled, meaning the businessmen, the cautious end-money investors, "but at the same time they're dying to get the good of the publicity. They want the hullabaloo. They know it's money in the bank and they can't let go." Melanie had been in the bungalow with them all the while, steeped in her book at her post in the corner, poker-faced and unperturbed and vigilant. There had been the last-minute awkwardness of getting around the child. But the time was passing The siesta would be ending, the hotel would be coming alive again, and if they were leaving, they had to be leaving soon. So they had gone drifting out in the sunlight; they had driven the three or four hundred yards across the deserted grounds to the rear of the main building, had left the car at the tree for Louis to pick up, and slipped furtively into the hall.

She moved freely in front of him. She had finished undressing and combing her hair, and was going to a closet, looking for a hanger for her dress. She made no fuss over her nakedness before him, either because she considered him of no account or because she was too careworn or because it was her way. In the film, filling the screen, she and most other actresses seemed large-sized and compelling, so that it invariably was a letdown and a surprise when you saw them close up in person; but the hot light from the blinds now, acting on her coloring, on the vivid red hair, gave her a flamboyance and she was larger than life and compelling again. Claris kept at a distance, continuing his surveillance. He struggled with his apprehensions, with his doubts and guilt and the basic pusillanimity in him, and so, as he studied her and dealt with his misgivings, there was a constraint, a resistance between them, nothing going on in the heavy torpor of the room and yet a tension existing, a shimmying encounter, a contest.

"You don't talk very much. You must be one of the silent ones," she said. "Some people talk, some people don't. Why is that?"

"I guess the people who don't talk just don't have anything to say," Claris said.

She held her shoulders straight, carrying her body with that clear-striding, forthright sexual quality they had and which they knew they had. It was the way they were put together; it was the bones in them. It was a readiness or acquiescence to use the body for all the pleasure it could give, a readiness they picked up from their mothers, in the Hollywood malt shops, out of the air. She had had a special upbringing. "I didn't come in on a wagonload of apples, you know," she had said to Claris in one of her bristling, unexpected declarations. Growing up in the Hollywood of her day, she had been exposed to the contagion from the studios. From all Claris had heard, it had been another time, everything closer to the studios in those days, the Los Angeles area still spread thin and relatively undeveloped, a third of what it was to become. The driving ambition among the youngsters, those who were pretty and spirited, was to wangle themselves into the studios somehow, to make the grade. They made the rounds while they were still at school, trying the different side entrances to the business—the small agents, small clubs, advertising conventions—and the sexual instinct was in play from the beginning, a commodity, something accepted as a matter of course. Claris thought of the fervor in the high-school sweet-shops, the beginning experimentings and first sallies; and thinking of those early times, he thought of the havoc in her now. When he had stayed on with her last evening in the bungalow after the fracas, when he had tried to console her and she had shut him off, he had seen the despair in her, the stubborn refusal to subside and come to terms with her misery. "Do I appall you? Is it too much?" she had said to him. "People get impatient with you for your woes and grief, but they insist on the right to their own sorrows—their personal hard luck is different and holy."

"For these shenanigans, to carry on a full-scale war with Case, for this you've got the strength," he had said to her. "For the work, no."

"If he thinks he's going to hold it over my head like a club, if he thinks he's going to lord it over me, he's got another think coming." She had meant the disgrace of her homecoming from England, the fiasco of the English marriage and all the other fiascos and debacles that Case had on her. His very appearance set her off. Claris remembered the jolt that had gone through her, how she had quivered the instant Case had stepped through the door and how she hadn't stopped trembling the whole time he had been in the bungalow with her. She couldn't bear the stance on him; it galled her to be reminded that she had been once led to rely on his bullyboy power for protection. She couldn't bear his harsh, swift gutter shots. He went straight to the point, with his thug's crudeness, making it impossible for her to twist away and hide, making her feel like nothing, she had said. Claris was puzzled by the persistence with which she kept herself bound to Case, hating him as she did, trembling with revulsion in his presence, and yet needing him and wanting him at hand. She needed and had to have him because he was hers. He had been with her over the years, had witnessed the succession of her follies and failures, was part of the shambles, all she had left, and he belonged to her and she wouldn't let him go. Case hadn't told it all when Claris had overheard him talking to Fannie about the early days, about the marriage proposal. Case had thrown it off—"She cried. 'Don't cry. I'm going.' She knew right then and there she was making a mistake of a lifetime—" but what he had omitted was the rapture, the subservience. "I think of you the first thing in the morning, the last thing at night when I fall asleep," Adele had quoted Case last evening when she was busy running him down and mocking him; and as Claris now followed her with his eyes, contending with her and with himself in this silent one-sided mental jujitsu he was going through, the thought wavered in his mind—the gift-giving, the head over heels courting and being in love, now all of it turned into detestation and venom.

She got on the bed, shifting her weight to one knee and then lying back, bringing up the other leg. The walls were thin, partitions—they could hear one or the other of the kitchen help walking about below; a voice rose up to them. The door was locked. Louis was sure to do what he could to steer the traffic away from the room, but in any case Claris didn't think the kitchen help presented much of a problem. They were a different breed, stolid, foreign born, unimpressionable, and even if they had noticed Claris's car in the delivery area, even if they discovered the room was being put to use and that it was Hogue, they would probably just pass it off. "Don't worry about the kitchen help," he said to Adele. "It doesn't mean anything to them. It wouldn't matter to them one way or the other." He finished placing his clothes on the chair. He sat on the bed and turned to her. She opened her arms to him, embraced and clasped him to her, taking him on, somebody on the road, whatever turned up, until the next full-blown, official romance came along. In the stickiness and travail, in the continuing tangle with Case, they took time out for themselves, letting go, as if this was a solution and a help. Claris responded to the pressure, winding through the ritual, the kisses, the fondling, the contriving of an illusion of love—that knavish, coward's thing people relentlessly do with one another. In the times with his wife, there were also kisses and endearments, as mystifying as these. There was the same mindless slippage, and then, later, the dead and gone sick hollowness, those cold moments of the night when you are alone and lost and the brute fear rears up before you and envelops you, when you perspire and don't know what you will ever do.

THEY WERE ON the freeway, miles out of the hotel-resort, speeding along through the open desert countryside, when they were caught in one of those periodic freeway traffic jams and knew they would be held up for at least another half hour or so. Instead of working back to the bungalow when they left the steward's room, because she didn't want to go back to the bungalow, because the motor was running, he had taken her for a drive. She had sat perched beside him all through the ride, not speaking, contrary and drawn into herself, acting out some new charade, and she didn't rouse now that they were stalled. It was a farm tractor, toppled over on its side, which was causing the breakdown. Claris didn't know what the tractor was doing there—heavy pieces of equipment weren't allowed on the freeway or at least were never seen—and in later years, when the recollection of the moment would come back to him, he always had trouble accounting for the tractor and wondered about it, except, of course, it was there, before his eyes, blocking the lanes. The cars drew up, packed in. Everything came to a halt. A lightness took hold. Car radios played. People stepped out of their cars, stared at one another in the sun and smiled, walking about where they normally wouldn't be walking. Claris looked down and saw the hard, murderous grain of the pavement concrete, the slits and abrasions, the concrete suddenly stationary and as if magnified. They had reached the crest of a hill when the traffic was stopped, and he had a long stretch of highway before him, now empty and inert. He saw the landscaped roadside banks—the spread of the portulaca, the ice plants, the wild California poppies on their high stems. The great stretch of the highway ahead of him, the peace and the kindness, the feel of the country air set up longings, making him think of the time when he had first come out to California to live, bringing back the nostalgia of first times, together with the rue or rebuke inherent in such reveries.

THE DRIVE MISCARRIED. Adele was seen. She was recognized, no doubt, during the tie-up, while the people were walking about, and she was seen in the car with some well set-up, athletic-looking, unidentified companion—a newcomer, a mysterious stranger, a new romance. Claris had known that sooner or later something would have to give, that she couldn't go on holding up the picture forever and that there would have to be a reckoning, and he had been consciously waiting all along for the blowoff to happen, half wanting it to happen, no matter how it might go and whatever it might do to him personally; but all the same the blowoff, when it came, caught him with a stinging surprise, and he could never have predicted the twisted, grating form it took. While he was still spinning over the highways with her, lulled and lending himself to the mood of the excursion, phones were ringing, men were moving in offices, alarms were being sounded. The persons who tipped off the reporters didn't know the newcomer in the car with her was Claris, her agent; as for the reporters, they were having a hard time of it keeping the weeks-old story on Hogue going. They were looking around for leads and developments, and so, when the tip came in, they leaped at the chance and were now avidly at work, beating up the new romance, the mysterious and unidentified stranger, for all the yardage and excitement they could get out of it. Claris had often watched the way the rumors seeped through the trade—people understood the gossip was hit and miss, concocted to fill up the columns, for the sake of the general commotion; and yet, by some peculiar aberration, perhaps because the business itself was flighty and laden with imponderables, these same individuals seized on the rumors, brooded on them, believed them and acted on them. That was why publicity agents assiduously invented and planted the items. "The fact that you see it in the papers doesn't necessarily mean it's untrue," the men in the industry reasoned. And so this new excitement—improvised on the spot, without responsibility or scruple, and yet, of course, not wide of the mark, coming at a time when Wigler was stretched out to the limit—was enough to bring on the final blow and send the whole project careening. The end-money investors stampeded. If Hogue was busy with a new romance, if she was off on another fling, then that explained the production delays, that meant she might very well take off for London or Paris and go out of sight again, and they wanted no part of the venture. Claris wasn't particularly worried as they rolled over the hotel

96

grounds on their return from the drive—if they were seen together now, it would only appear that he had driven her somewhere on business, on an errand, as agents did with their clients—but when they reached the cottage, Case and Fannie were waiting inside as a reception committee, and the upheaval was on. Adele had darted on ahead into the bungalow, and when Claris came around the car and followed after her, not thinking anything was amiss, he walked straight into the thick of the scuffle, Case and Adele already at it. Melanie was there. The twins were underfoot. Fannie had fed them and was trying now, with Melanie's help, to herd them off to bed and out of the way, and Claris weaved through the disorder, taking up his place at the wall and listening. Wigler had left for the city earlier in the day. He had been called to a bankers' meeting and had been fiddling with the loan executives, pleading, placating, getting out from under, giving his heart-felt assurances, those guarantees which he could never hope to fulfill, when the blow had fallen on him. He was lunging after the end-money people at this moment, and everything now depended on what Case could do with Adele.

Claris held back, again on the sidelines, again trying not to draw attention to himself, the fright pulsing through him—the old, dismal quickening of all the other near misses, escapes, reprieves—and as he watched and waited, he wondered if he would scrape through this time again, if there would be another reprieve. He wouldn't have known how to face Case and was grateful that he didn't have to. He stared at Adele. He had been with her a while ago in the steward's room. The remembrance of what had gone on there between them was still with him, in the front of his mind. He thought the signs must be written all over his face, but she didn't show a trace of awareness, and he wondered how they did it. For them, the sexual act, once done, was over, forgotten. You saw this bland, cool acceptance in young girls as they sat in restaurants, looking at menus—a certain instinctive reliance, a kind of birthright, which they acknowledged and made use of and on which they seemed to set no great store. She was in the same yellow sleeveless dress, the same stockings, which Claris had seen her take off and put on again. She repulsed Case with a total intensity, her face shiny and perspired, not caring how she looked, not troubled now by that heightened susceptibility to perspiration which distressed and burdened women of her florid coloring. Case rasped at her. He wanted to get off word to Wigler as soon as possible. He wanted her to start back for the studio immediately, to stop the rumors and save Wigler before it was altogether too late, if it wasn't altogether too late already. "There is no time! There is no time!" He was baffled by the obstinancy in her. He was exasperated from the long wait at the hotel—"I laid around all day like a fool, watching the chauffer, while you go off on a drive!" The expedition over the desert brought back memories of the other jaunts and forays, and he pitched into her recklessly, upbraiding her now for her shiftlessness, for those old, wanton, impulsive one-time engagements. She hit back promptly, reminding him now he used to spy on her. She drew savage pictures of him at the phone, calling up people, asking anxiously who was with her, who had gone into her trailer dressing-rooms on the set, if she had left the set and with whom and for how long. She turned and walked away from him.

"If it's not one thing it's the other, always a crisis," Fannie said, coming out of the bedroom, some of the children's clothing in her hands. She was in a wretched mood. She had been in and out all along, had been undressing the twins and had more work to do with them, but she had heard enough to know that things were going badly, that Adele wasn't packing and leaving for the studio. "If you held a pistol to her head, if you turned yourself inside out," Fannie said. Adele had the bathroom door open, and while the actress stood there at the medicine-chest mirror, washing the dust of the drive off her face and running a comb through her hair, Fannie and her ex-husband jawed away at each other, talking at cross purposes, not seeing each other.

"Later on she'll complain and have it against us that we didn't insist and let her do what she wanted to do," Case said.

"So what? What's the tragedy?" Fannie shouted. "Let her do nothing and look at television all day like everybody else." Fannie knew how critical the moment was, was sick about the ruin Adele was bringing down on herself, and it hurt her as much as it did Case, but she saw no way out of the impasse. "He's got a yen for her," she said. "If you want to make it with them, you have to call them up in the middle of the night. You have to give them trouble left and right and then they're happy."

"Were you the guy?" Case asked, switching to Claris. He meant was Claris the man who had been seen in the car with her, the reason for the present speculations and flare-up. Case quickly put it together and saw for himself how the misunderstanding had happened; he realized Adele didn't have another man somewhere, that there hadn't been time for a new romance. "Why did you do that?" he asked Claris, blunt and harassed. "Why did you encourage her? Didn't you have better sense than that? You're supposed to help around here, not make it worse."

He swerved off. Adele had come out of the bathroom, and he went crashing back to her, set on convincing her and making her do his bidding by the force of his will, because he was telling her. He was tied to her. She was warm to him, supple, necessary. Claris had watched the old-timers in the projection rooms at the studios, men grizzled and heavy-eyed, quietly appraising some new girl on film there in a screen test. "She's soft, not like these tough babes you see around, everything on the line," a man would say, searching out that indefinable, essentially feminine appeal that worked in the movie houses, that drew these men in their personal lives, too. Adele had this softness for Case, knew she had it, recognized his need for her, counted on it, and took advantage of it to spite and bedevil him in every way she could think of. He was arguing with her now that she had to work whether she was up to it or not up to it, that she had no choice, that this was no time for temperamental fireworks—she couldn't afford to be temperamental. It developed that she had had hard commitments on her when she had flown off and made her international marriage. Claris had heard about the commitments at the office, but he hadn't known too much about them, and no one had ever told him of the big sums that had been advanced on the promise of these pictures in the future—money which she was liable for and had to make good on and which apparently had been squandered in the year and a half she had lived abroad. Case bore away at her. Yes, he had spied on her. He knew all about the winter skiing trips, the high-toned places, Monaco, the yachts, the being in the right places at the right time with the right collection of snobs—as if it mattered, as if anybody cared. "What do you think, they were standing three deep on the sidewalk, waiting to hear all about you?" He knew the hopes she had put on the splurge, on the plush life and the traveling around; he knew how much it had meant to her to have them all back home impressed with her and envious. "If you stopped the first ten people that came walking down the street and asked them, would they know what you were talking about?" He talked about the life and death struggle that went on at the mooring basin in Monte Carlo, how they killed themselves there to get the favored mooring posts, to get their yachts anchored up close to the yachts of the reigning muck-a-mucks, so that they could all be one big, important mob.

"How he's got it all down pat," Adele said. "How he knows every little detail. He can't get over it."

"Come on, don't be like that," he said, trying to shake her up, to hurry her over the hard feelings of the past. "Have a little understanding. It's not as much as you think it is. You don't have to hold every last little thing against me." He explained that Wigler was on the ropes, that she was in no position to take a bustup, that the conditions in the industry weren't what she thought they were, that there were the children. He went charging at her, out of exasperation and anxiety falling more and more into that overbearing, pugnacious manner of his, that gross bullyboy show of muscle, which she couldn't stand and which only reinforced her determination to resist him. Claris could see her nerving herself up against him, how she fired herself to sustain her fury. It was probably one of those spasms when, carried away as she was, she nevertheless knew what she was doing and could stop herself at any point, but deliberately chose not to and forged on ahead. She had been through the mill, had been brought along, and knew now what she once didn't know; she understood the publicity had gone awry, that the picture was being shot out from under her, that she would be isolated, blacklisted by the trade. And yet the old injuries, the remembered ugly scenes and humiliations still stood between them, keeping her alive and blinding her to every practical considera-

tion. Claris could see why she had had to have the pro-
cession of husbands—so that she could assert herself
over Case and keep him off, so that he wouldn't be able to
tear her down.

"Don't look at me like that. Don't give me those
faces," Case said to her. "You know the things you got
against me are the things you did. It's not me. It's you."
He started again, trying to reason with her. "You
don't have to be afraid. No one's against you." And then
it swept over him. He broke loose. "You got a mania in
you, a poison—whatever's no good for you you got to
have. You're so racked up and worked over you don't
know the day of the week. The only time you know what's
happening to you is when you're facing the cameras,
and that's the one thing you have to run away from.
You don't know how to handle yourself or live, and
nobody can straighten you out, nobody can tell you
what to do." It was all up with Wigler. The picture was
doomed. Case could see he had been laboring for nothing.
She wasn't driving back to Culver City. She wasn't
going to do a sudden about-face and fall in line with
him and his wishes at this late stage. But what stuck in
his throat, what had been gnawing in him all along and
had started him off, was the bringing back of those
desert weekend afternoons, the times on the phone and
the hurt, and all that had gone on since.

"Do you call it a life, does it make sense—marrying
them and then throwing them out, every year a turnover?
You come dragging back, more dead than alive, forced

to face the music, and you have to start patching yourself up all over again." He cast up at her the squalls, the wretched, drawn-out contests, each one like a campaign, which she had taken on in her time, wallowed in, and had never seemed able to avoid; he touched on one hideous, thoroughly publicized botch of a marriage, to a man far too old for her, a man who had passed on while she was still married to him. "How many times? Go over the list—the divorces, the battles, fighting them tooth and nail, fighting them to a finish, and then having them die on you, this too to worry about, this too to have on your head and carry around with you. Wasn't it always the same, all your life—running out whenever the brainstorm hit you, always wanting, always scared to death you weren't getting your full share? You went shooting off on one foot, chasing the rainbows, dumping everything no matter who got hurt in the process." He rammed home the devastating indictments, recalling people dead and buried, people jettisoned on the way; he recalled that mass of ignominies, the blunders, the biting acts of stupidity, the chances failed and ruined— that dreary clutter which assails the mind as we lie abed in the dark, never to be redeemed or assuaged, so that we sleep every other night. "You don't care what you do to yourself, how you use yourself up. You don't stop to think what you can stand. And it all goes on in a gold-fish bowl—the courts in Santa Monica, the reporters standing around, everything in the open." He reached back to the beginnings, to the rat-trap backstage dressing-

room areas, to the cheap club dates, when, in her eager-
ness to break in, she had mixed with the low life of the
business, the hangers-on, the felons, the spoilers.

He stopped short. He wrenched out of his tirade.
"Who needs it? She's old. Who wants her? She was
a hula girl when radio was big." He suddenly saw himself, raging and excited over something that was past
and meant nothing to him. It was out of him. He was
through with her. If she wanted to wreck herself, then
let her—what was it to him? "It was my fault. It was
her fault. Who knows who started what, how it began.
I didn't do enough for her. I was a mug. I didn't talk
right." He pulled away and started for the door.

"Hello and goodbye!" Fannie said. She was out of
the children's bedroom. She had been standing there for
some time, listening to the outburst, too embittered to
interfere. She knew it would do no good to interfere, that
the picture was gone and the damage done, and it also
went roiling in her to see the passion in Case, how he
took on. "No fool like an old fool, still going for girls,"
she said, grinding out the words. "He pecks his jaw
out and holds his head high in the air to kill the double
chin. His fingers are all stuck together from the arthritis
and he can't open his hand but he's still got young
ideas." Case's left hand was crippled, the fingers remarkably shriveled and wedged in at the palm, a de-
formity Claris hadn't been aware of until Fannie now
referred to it.

"What's going to happen to her?" Case blurted at her,

cutting in, and for a while they hacked back and forth at the door, Case wrangling with his ex-wife, talking about the fix Adele was in, the debts, the children. She was broke, he said. The parade was passing her by. If she managed to live down the mess, if it ever did blow over, how many more cracks out of the box did she have in her, how many more pictures was she good for? Four, five? "She's all dried out from the dieting. Who's going to want to see her? There's a whole flock of them coming up, new ones with names nobody ever heard of."

"It was a different story when she first came down the pike, snapping her garters," Fannie said, giving up, seeing the end of it. She knew everything Case said was true, that the outlook was black, and there was nothing to be gained by standing at the door and arguing. "The goddammed coronaries, the heart attacks and cancer— they're dropping like flies, everywhere you look, and he's still in contention. The showplace house there with the private driveway," she said, going back to the early days, when they had come to California, when he had been enthralled with the movie elite and had gone running after them. "When they came to the house, he couldn't do enough to entertain them. Whatever they wanted—chicken, chicken; steak, steak—he ran a restaurant!" Case was gone. He had slammed out, leaving to place his call to Wigler, to do whatever could be done in the debacle. Fannie was gathering up some laundry—she still had the children's clothes in her hands when she had come out of the bedroom—and Claris waited while she roamed around the room, picking up a pair of socks, a white piqué hat, whatever needed washing, and prepared to follow out after her former husband.

If he could have helped her or comforted her, he would have spoken up, but anything he could think to say would be fatuously out of keeping and would only aggravate the misery in her, so he kept silent. Back at the agency, when they had a hard case on their hands, some actress who was giving trouble, he had watched the men ducking for cover, shuffling the actress from one to the other—"You take her. I had her all day yesterday. You sit with her. You take her to dinner." But here, the way it had worked out, the way he had unwittingly fallen into this morass, the responsibility was all his. He was bound. He couldn't fob her off even if there was anyone to fob her off on, and he could see no way of extricating himself. There wasn't a sound from the back of the cottage. The twins, played out and exhausted after the day's helling around, were sleeping regally on the big, oversized double bed—they had the master bedroom, while Adele and Melanie shared the twin beds in the other room. Melanie didn't come out, sparing them this once, probably too frightened and desolate in there to be able to maintain that poise of hers, that persevering, resolute deadpan calm. "You make it a practice never to look back," Adele said. "You can't go around thinking of all the horrible damn things you did all your life or that you got yourself into, so the result is in the end you lose touch with reality. You become a zombie. You don't know if the thing you're hitting yourself over the head with actually ever happened to you or if you imagined it or dreamed it or if it happened to somebody else and you just heard about it or read it in the paper." She was on a tear; it would be one of those grainy vigils which had become the pattern of his visits with her—at the sunbaked studio dressing-room apartment, at the hotel in Beverly Hills, now here in the bungalow at the resort—when he stood by, saying nothing, not supposed to speak, while she came on with her hard, self-despoiling knock, delivering those flaunting, wild statements and admissions as though he wasn't in the room or didn't count. She was rapping up, for a change, on the fashionable women-guests, the second and third wives with their bored, intelligent eyes. "You can bet they never have to second-guess themselves or have regrets. They play it close, keep it all to themselves, never tell you a dream. The first thing they do, the minute they get out of bed in the morning, is to step on the scales and weigh themselves, like a religious rite." When she was thirteen and fourteen, she had once told Claris, she used to read the women's magazines as they appeared each month. In order to make more of herself and get beyond the local neighborhood improvisations—the homemade tricks, the butterfly kisses, that is, the young girls flicking their eyelashes against the cheeks of their companions— in order to go beyond these attainments and get the jump on the other girls in her group, she would faithfully study the pages of the large-circulation magazines to learn what was done, what was not done, what was worn, to pick up clues, to absorb the explicit sexual information these publications offered. And thinking of her at those glossy pages, he could understand why she compulsively chipped away at the stylish ladies, with their silky contentment, and felt about them as she did, however they had come by their expertise, whatever their beginnings were. She ran on, talking about weight problems, how with her, when the dieting got by her, the weight would go straight to her thighs. With some people the weight settled in the rear, with others it was the abdomen—with her, the thighs. She spoke of a husband of hers who got a big kick out of her suddenly thick, Irish washerwoman's thighs, who was always after her to pass up her diet and indulge herself, who always had his hands on the thighs and the rest of her. She spoke of the lascivious binges, the intensive, sequestered sexual proclivities of husbands, and wives, and the carnivals she'd been on. "It goes on like a running fit," she said. She described the pursuits, the getting out of pantics, the bouts on the hall landings, in the guest room, talking as Claris sometimes heard women, past a certain point in life, batting out the phrases, without embellishment, with a coarse, unminding directness.

"If I could do the work, if I could get myself on the set, I wouldn't be here in the first place, did that ever occur to you?" she said, lashing at him, not that he had said anything to her, but because she knew this was what he wanted her to do, because this was the only way out for her. "You have to go in like a bank robber." She railed against the work she did, reviling it—because of its shifting, tantalizingly elusive nature and because she had never been able to beat it. "Every time you finish a picture, you have to go into business and start from scratch all over again. You don't know what it is when you can't do it, when you come up empty. They think somebody tells you something about breathing, that you have to wash your hair once a day every day, and that's all there is to it. If it's that easy, then why don't they try it? You stand there, trying to remember what you once did, what it was you once had, trying to get it back, while all the time you know perfectly well you were never that good and had nothing in particular to begin with." She was racing, saying whatever came into her head, and what was odd, what Claris couldn't fail to notice and what moved and disturbed him was the manner of her, that even as she ranted and tumbled the words out, there was still a holding back, an uncertainty and guilt— the same lack of nerve and abiding mortification that rode her and made it impossible for her to go in front of the cameras and meet people.

"Why do you want to make yourself unhappier than you have to be," Claris said to her. He tried to restrain her, to break the rhythm of her hysteria. "It's not as bad as you think it is. Take my word for it. You'll sleep on it. You'll wake up in the morning and you'll wonder what it was all about, why you let yourself get so upset."

She shook him off. "What do you know about it?

110

What are you pushing yourself into this for? What are you trying to tell me, that you really care, that you're crazy in love with me? Why should people love me— because of my lousy self-centered misery and perpetual troubles? I've been there before, people latching on, with all the good words, fattening off me, getting themselves contracts."

She drove at him. She let him know exactly how desperate her situation was. She told him everything now. The dazzling high life, the fascinating social swirl hadn't been as it appeared. She told him about her husband and the speedy, good-looking crowd he had run with. She told Claris of their sport, their games and antics, the way they had systematically wheedled the money out of her, using one excuse or the other. Claris floundered. Harry Case had talked about the commitments and the money she had squandered, but now Claris began to see why the man had been so angered and bitten with vexation. The racing stables, the plush traveling around, the trips to Monto Carlo, the splurge and show on which she had set such high hopes and which were to make everyone impressed with her and envious—it had all been her money. Her fine aristocrat of a husband had had no money. He was completely dependent on his father for support, and his father, the famous English sporting duke, with his estates and great renown, was the tightwad of the country. Everyone knew it. He wouldn't give up a penny. She had footed the bills, had underwritten the parties. The eighteen months' sojourn, from start to finish, had cost her four hundred thousand dollars.

Claris was staggered by the enormity of the sum, by the hopeless, useless waste. "How could you let them do that? Didn't you know what was going on?"

"Because I didn't know better! Because I was a fool! What was I going to do—come back here where I had all this waiting for me? I had to stick it out," she explained to him, imploring. "I had to make a go of it. I sat there— half the time I didn't know what they were talking about. I was afraid to open my mouth. I'm crazy, don't you understand—looking in the looking-glass crazy. Go ahead—you have all the advice to give. Tell me what to do. Tell me everything is hunky-dory."

She pushed past him and went out of the room. The first hard jolt of dismay had subsided, and a kind of panic now took its place. The lights were all on, as they always were in that place, and he stood in the glare, his mind working and grasping, trying to scrounge out an escape for himself, going over the field, knowing he would do what he wanted to do, what it was in him to do. For a moment, he marveled at the tenacity in her these last weeks, fighting and standing them off, all the time knowing the ground was cut out from under her and that she hadn't a chance. She was blown. She couldn't work. It was all shutting down on her and there was no telling what she might do. They killed themselves, putting matches to their nightgowns, taking the tablets and huddling in some dingy, Godforsaken closet, going there to hide and die as for some reason they did—and all he knew was that he didn't want to be on the scene any longer, that he had to get away. He had gone as far as he had been able to go; he had done the best that it had been in his nature to do.

H̶E LOITERED in the stiff, gray living room of his home. The sun hadn't burned through the morning mist, the morning damp—the maritime breezes, they called it here. The help—the cook, the baby's nurse—were up and about; Claris could hear them somewhere in the house. He was dressed, shaved and showered, all rigged out for the day's work at the office, except that he had no proper day's work and he didn't know what lay ahead. It was hours too early to start for the office. He had had no clear notion of what he was doing or going to do when he had bolted the resort and driven the hundred miles back to town the night before. He had decided that he would have to play it as it came, riding his luck, seeing how it broke. He was on the run. When the office opened this morning, they would be dealing with the overnight developments; there would be meetings, Meyerson and Cottrell would be having Prescott on the carpet; and Claris wanted to be in the room there when Prescott started double-talking his way out of the jam and reported to the bosses. With the papers making

114

a business out of the brand-new romance, with the columnists' legmen shooting around to hunt up the identity
of the mysterious newcomer—that is, in short, looking for
him—Claris was on thin ice, and he intended to stay
close to Prescott all day long, clamping down on him and
making sure he didn't spill. Claris saw that in scuttling
off and running out on the actress, he had at least helped
himself to that extent—he was much better off here on
the spot in town, looking out for his interests, than he
would have been at the resort.

To fill in the time, to get a breathing spell and steady
himself, because there was the three hours' difference
in time and it wouldn't be too early for her, he called his
wife in New York. He got her at her grandparents'
house. They talked, Claris speaking in that flat, idle tone
which it always astonished him he was able to assume
with her at will. "What are you doing there, Barbara?"
he chided her as they went along. She had been gone a
little longer than it seemed to him they had either of them
anticipated, and, in the natural way, because it was more
or less indicated, he felt obliged to put up a protest,
reproaching her for the delay in returning. There was
a pause. She was slow in replying. The exchange became uneven, and in another instant, without warning,
the respite, the breathing spell, came to an end. "Don't
you think you ought to be thinking about getting back?
Don't you think the baby needs you?" he asked her.

"I want to think things out," she said, faraway, in her
child's voice.

His first instinct was to shy off. "What do you mean, you want to think things out? What's there to think out about?" he said, hustling it, acting as though he hadn't quite heard her, as though he couldn't possibly understand what she meant. He changed the subject, talked about the house, the baby, and brought the conversation to a finish. He hung up. He sat on the couch, wondering what she could have heard or knew, or, as was more likely the case, what some member of that tight-packed, protective family of hers had heard. So far as he could tell, everything had been at peace with him and his wife when she had left on the trip and when he had talked to her the times on the phone, so whatever happened surely had to do with Adele and it had to have happened recently, in the last day or two. He went over the people at the studio, the people at the resort, the steward Louis—he couldn't see how any of them could have given him away. For a moment he wondered if anything could have broken through last night, if that was it—if in some way the reporters had got to Prescott and Prescott had already spilled.

The baby's nurse came passing through—the nurse who had worked in a number of houses in the area and was battle-wise, who had a pretty good idea of how it was with Claris in that household; whenever she spoke to Claris about his wife, she had always referred to her as Missus Claris, hitting the missus. She had a jumpy, resentful nature, was constitutionally dissatisfied, and Claris normally avoided her as much as he could, but in his quandary he turned to her—after all, she had been on the phone with his wife throughout the visit back east. He told her frankly about the phone call. He asked her what she knew, if his wife had said anything to her.

"Why didn't you ask her? If the remark puzzled you, you should have asked her what she meant and had it out," the nurse said, fussing, all at once unstrung and combative.

"Do you know anything?" Claris said.

"No, you should have asked her. I don't see why I should be in the middle. Go to the spare room," the nurse said, suddenly getting the words out. "Try the spare room. Maybe you'll be enlightened." Claris looked at her, dumbfounded, not understanding what the spare room had to do with it. "The mattress, the mattress, under the mattress," the nurse said, and left.

He found the packet of letters. He knew he was being mocked, but he didn't know what to make of this mockery. A moment ago he had been on the run, twisting and calculating, worrying about Prescott and the gossip columnists, and suddenly he was in the clear. The shoe was on the other foot. His wife didn't have the goods on him; he had the goods on her. He undid the packet, untying the candybox ribbon with which she had carefully kept the letters bound and secure in their hiding place under the mattress. The letters went back over a period of months. She had had them addressed to a friend of hers—that was how she had managed the correspondence. Claris knew the man, the maitre d', one of the partners, of a mid-Manhattan restaurant—Claris and his wife had always gone to the place when they were in New York, and had been made welcome. Claris had consistently deceived his wife, phoning in he'd be late, that he was called away, dodging and going through the strategems, and it now appeared his wife had been busy with undertakings of her own. In the first flush of the discovery, while he was trying to absorb the impact and was still off balance, a mean, eager spurt of relief actually went through him—that he had gotten off and not been caught. And then the full sickening force of the mockery overtook him. He saw what a disaster he had made of himself. Amazingly, at that moment, his wife became dear to him. He longed for her. A homesickness seized him, now that he had come to an ending, that the time with his wife was over and completed. He saw his wife on her back. He wanted to hit out and take revenge. It infuriated him to think of the maitre d' having his hands on her, having his chance now at the fortune that went with her—the supermarkets, the real-estate holdings. Claris told himself that it wasn't right, not after what he had gone through, not after what he had done to himself. He thought of his in-laws, those stout-built men, so smug and indulgent and circumspect. He could hear them making up the package when his wife first brought home the news that she wanted to marry him. "You want it, baby? All right, you got it," they must have said. And then they had proceeded with the apparatus, tying up the money, keeping everything separate and at arms' length, figuring that she would tire of him in a few years and that nothing would be lost. They hadn't even considered him for the famliy business, disposing of him, instead, in a five-minute telephone call to someone they knew at the agency.

He spent the next half hour or so packing two large suitcases, cleaning out his suits, his shirts, his shoes, and the rest of it. He wanted the shelves and closets to be bare, to look bare and stripped and strewn. The cook and nurse probably knew, or at any rate would soon know, what he was doing. He didn't care how it appeared to them or what they would say to his wife when she called. He put the packet of letters into his pocket. He wasn't letting them go. He carried the two bulky suitcases out to the car in the garage, and then drove from the house, in the western part of Los Angeles, through the curves of Sunset Boulevard as it wound around the base of the Hollywood Hills, deep into the Hollywood area until he reached the Athletic Club. He checked into the club-hotel and had himself an address, a place of his own. The club building was drenched in the California sun, that persistent downpour of heat which soaked through the brick of the building, into the room, into the drapes and upholstery. Claris didn't take time to open a window. In the still dead air, he fixed on the name of a lawyer, got the number out of the book, and stood at the phone, insisting on an immediate, early morning appointment. It was important for him not to stop; it was as though he knew that whatever was to be done had to be done without a halt. He could remember, or thought he could easily remember once he tried, other instances where families, similarly placed in a predicament of this sort, quickly came to a settlement, without going through the scandal of a courtroom trial, and he didn't want any indecisiveness or temporizing to weaken his resolve.

He drove to the lawyer's and was led into the private office. There were abominations not to be acknowledged by the mind, but the astounding thing was that you went right ahead and did them. He wasn't a monster. He loved his child. He stood in the office, well-groomed, presentable, with his clean, athletic lines, nominally there to ask for advice, to explain the circumstances he found himself in and to see what legal redress he had. But he knew and the lawyer knew that what he was after was to use the child—the custody of the child, the threat of a courtroom fight—to wheedle or blackmail a lump cash settlement out of the family. The lawyer never changed expression. He heard Claris out, unsurprised, unflustered. Claris had often observed these people, so fond and benign in the bosom of their families—good husbands, good fathers and uncles, respectable, mild—and yet, in the business way, when the pinch was on, capable of criminalities and devices of which Claris and his kind knew nothing. In his idiocy, Claris had gone to a lawyer who was one of theirs—where else could Claris have gone, what other lawyers did he know about? Later on, when at odd moments the events of that feverish morning flickered back to him, he would wonder what he had thought he was doing. He would be honestly at a loss to understand the mania that had possessed him. In the heat and impetus of his bungling wrath, there might have been a logic to his behavior, but he hadn't a hope of getting by with his feckless, far-out scheme, and even in his derangement he must have known it. He knew how ruthless his in-laws could be. He knew they handled these holdups and worse every month, that they didn't take alarm, were geared for them, had the required resources and connections. He wasn't in the same league with these people and should never have begun. The lawyer—Claris didn't know how or when it had come about—had shifted from his desk during the interview and was standing now at the door, holding it open.

"All right, all right, go along," the lawyer said, not wanting to enter into a discussion or extend himself, anxious to get Claris moving. "They'll cover you with it until you won't see daylight. They'll take everything away from you and leave you flat as a pancake," he told Claris, and got him out the door.

He went straight to his office from the lawyer's— possibly because he had been heading for the agency before he had been interrupted, because he was panicked and didn't know where else to go. Most of the staff were out in the field, at the different studios, at this time of day. The floor was empty, the halls dim and cool, and he walked past the reception girl at the switchboard and was able to get to his room without being stopped. He sat in the cubicle, routed and demeaned, the ceiling pressing down on his head. He wondered what would become of him. He knew you were lost in this town if you didn't belong, if they didn't want you around, and in one senseless sweep, for reasons that were beyond him and would always be beyond him, he had kicked out every support from under him. In his agitation, he thought of his mother—he didn't know what he would say to her, how he would explain it. He didn't know what she and her husband would do without the weekly check he gave them. The phone rang. He was chopped. Claris couldn't believe it—he had been gone from the lawyer's no more than twenty minutes in all, and already the machinery was grinding. There was no formal notification. They had left it to the switchboard girl to tell him he was through, that his close-out check would be in the mail. "Sorry," the girl said. She ran on, "First they wanted you, tracking you all over, high and low, and then suddenly—forget it, hands off him." Claris was muddled—he didn't know why they had had to track him high and low, what the great rush had been—but when he tried to query the girl, she turned hostile and aloof, as they did when they knew you were down and the knock was in.

Prescott walked into the cubicle, tipped off, no doubt, by the switchboard girl. Working with the bosses all morning as he had, he knew that Claris had been dropped and was no longer with the agency, but that didn't deter him. He came at Claris, complaining and spoiling—Claris had let him down; he was on the spot; he had the whole mess to clean up now by himself; they were all on him and he could lose his job—where was she? What had Claris done with her? Where had he taken her?

Claris didn't know what he wanted or was talking about. He half rose from the chair to shove him out of the room. And then it came to him. Prescott explained what had happened. Adele wasn't at the resort. She had disappeared. With everything at the last failing her, she had done the only thing she knew how to do and had run off again, except that this time no one knew where she was. Claris saw why the bosses had been tracking him down. They thought he had her. That was what Prescott had told them. Prescott, with his thief's brain, had taken it for granted that Claris would be still latching on, that he would never willingly let her go or walk away from him. Prescott realized by now that Claris had nothing to do with the disappearance.

"If she's not with you, then where is she?" Prescott jabbered. The hired chauffeur she had brought up to the resort with her was still on the place. If the chauffeur hadn't driven her, then how did she get away? Who had driven her? Where had she gone?

"You want I should help you find her, Dick?" Claris said, straight-faced, leaden.

"What kind of a crack do you call that?" Prescott said. "That's no contribution. You had the responsibility."

"You think I ought to make amends?" Claris continued. "You want me to make a contribution?"

Prescott started to answer, saw the look on Claris's face, thought better of what he was doing, and suddenly began backing out of the room. Claris let the lunatic gargoyle look fade from his face. He sat at the desk. The heat and tumult were gone. The megrims had him—the rale, the ancient basic horror. When he had gone to the lawyers, yes, it was mania, a compulsive fury to break loose and bring everything down, anything he cared to tell himself—at bottom, and he knew it, he wanted the money. When he had slipped out on the actress, he hadn't admired himself; now that he was going back, the offense was all the greater. He was going back to her because she was alone; because he had no excuses, since it made no difference now whether anyone knew he was mixed up with her or didn't know; because he was destitute and adrift and had nothing going for him; because Prescott, with his thief's brain and scurrilous assumptions, was right.

T HE HOTEL-RESORT, when he reached it, lay still, curiously unchanged and as he had left it, the great 117-degree afternoon desert heat sifting down and holding everything fast. There was no outward sign of disturbance to be detected, whatever was going on with Case and Fannie, however they were searching for Adele and worrying over her disappearance. She was in the steward's quarters over the kitchen. Claris knew where she was. He had put it together and guessed where she had gone the minute he had heard the hired chauffeur hadn't disappeared from the hotel along with her. She had run out of hiding places and retreats; she simply had nowhere she could have told the chauffeur to drive her. Claris understood the compulsion in her to remove herself from sight and withdraw from contact with the world. That was at the center of her malady. That was the reason why at periodic intervals one star or the other, without warning or explanation, would suddenly scuttle a picture in mid-production and go hurtling off.

125

Overloaded and beyond themselves, appalled by their inability to do what they thought they were expected to do, they craved to pull the shutters down, to give up, to stick themselves in some out of the way corner and let it all go by without them. It wasn't temperament or a taste for sensation, the motives commonly ascribed. Now that she had come to the end of her gyrations, with the reporters ready to flock in on her because of the so-called new romance, she needed a refuge more desperately than before, and so Claris had this tricky, onerous arrangement on his hands, the actress stashed away in Louis's room right there in the midst of them on the premises, while they hunted far and wide for her. Wigler was sunk. That remarkable resilience which carried him from crisis to crisis, which was his stock in trade, wouldn't serve him any longer. His backers had dispersed and he would never group them together again, with all his enduring reliance and tenacity. But for Adele the outlook wasn't necessarily hopeless. It was the unforgivable sin in the industry to bankrupt a production, but Claris had seen cases where actresses, in a similar situation, had nevertheless managed to extricate themselves and come back. It was a matter of time, of waiting for the scandal to die down, as in some miraculous way it often did, of counting on the indefatigable resilience and optimism which were the stock in trade of other producers as well as of Wigler. That was why the stars probably allowed themselves these tantrums in the first place, Claris thought, because they knew they could survive their excesses and be forgiven. The commitments she had for future pictures were all to the good; in order to recoup on their investments and on the advances paid out to her, the producers would be lured in spite of themselves to go on with their projects, so she already had one foot in the door. Claris knew enough of the business to handle the studio details, to make deals and front for her. He could provide a genuine support and service, he told himself, and as he tooled the car over the grounds, he kept testing these reflections in his mind, putting them into an order, really to fortify himeslf, so that when he saw her, he would come prepared, would have a realistic, plausible program of action to offer her, and be able to give her heart and convince her.

At the parking area, he caught the yardman on his rounds and got him to go up to the main building to find Louis for him. Claris stayed close to the car. There were some hundreds of yards between the parking area and the entrance leading to the rooms above the kitchen, and he wasn't going to go out in the open on his own. By this time, with the total breakdown of the picture and the alarm over Adele's disappearance, he knew the word had already gone out on him, and the last thing he wanted now was to stumble into the Cases, into one of the reporters or whoever else might be around, and get himself involved in some ghoulish, awkward encounter. Louis came down promptly. The steward had followed the course of Claris's difficulties with the actress ever since they had come to the hotel. He knew what was at stake, how in the nature of these things a relationship with a star of Hogue's standing could pay big dividends, and what Claris was angling for. By a peculiar twist of values, since Louis was also on the outside looking in, constantly in the company of men on the fringes hoping to catch on, men like Pepi Straeger for instance, he saw the problem from their point of view, and in the gravity of the present situation facing Claris, the steward held out a steady, earnest flow of sympathy, a sympathy which palled on Claris and which he consciously tried to discourage. The actress had been in the room since early morning, Louis said. She had presented herself at the door. Louis had heard the knock, at six in the morning, and there she was—that was how it had happened. Louis hadn't intended to do anything until he had heard from Claris, but he had started to wonder, he said, the time passing as it did and no sign of Claris.

"Don't you have to look out for yourself?" Claris said. "Can't you get in trouble?"

Louis shrugged off the risks to himself. He was alone, without a family to care for, or aspirations—what could they do to him? That was the advantage of being a man in his position, he said in his stiff, fine undertones. He went to scout the lay of the land. Claris walked up the rise of ground which separated the parking lot from the hotel proper. He waited at the crest there until Louis gave the signal, and then strode across the clearing to the kitchen area, went past Louis at the door, and safely got into the hallway.

She was badly worn, as he might have imagined she would be after the long hours spent by herself. She had left the door unlocked and had obviously been waiting for him to come to her—who else would have known where she was? She had to have him, or somebody, with her all the time, because without a man or husband to dance attendance on them they became woebegone and frantic, but now that he was with her and she had him, he could see from the outset that it was impossible to do anything for her. He stood away, letting her rip at herself. He wondered what she would have done if he hadn't come by. He thought of the other scrapes he had been in, the preposterous backstairs maneuverings, the harum-scarum last-minutes escapes. "Take a chance. Are you afraid?" a woman had once said to him in a bar, leading him on, baiting him, and he knew he was through with infidelities and hairbreadth escapes for a good time to come. He couldn't talk to Adele. This was no time to trot out his long-range plans for the future, to show her how they could make it famously as a team together, Claris zealously safeguarding her interests and running interference for her. "One of those," she said. She was referring to herself, to the way she looked and the impression she knew she must be making on him. "You see them—these overwrought ladies with hyperthyroid eyes, going from pillar to post, the lipstick smeared on their mouths. People throw themselves around and don't know what to do with themselves." She looked about her, seeing herself in the Filipino steward's quarters, buried

129

in this unlikely setting while the hunt was on for her. "Nobody knows they're crazy until somebody officially comes and tells them," she said. She was frazzled by the break with Case. She hadn't expected it. Whatever she thought of him and in spite of the venomous, disgraceful jibes she threw out at him when they quarreled, he had been someone to fall back on, to return to, to blame for the errors she had made and the way things had gone. So long as she had him, she could still feel desired somewhere, that she was worth desiring, and now that this familiar support, which she had thought would always be there, was taken away from her, she was bereft, forced to deal by herself with the miseries that plagued her.

She fidgeted, her face freckled and pinkish and perspiring in the strong light that came off the walls, the ceiling, the bare boards of the floor, and suffused the room with its solid heat. She half lay in the chair, her legs bent at the knees and jutting out before her, the body let go, the body which she treated with such an impatient contempt and which she felt had betrayed her. Claris saw the roundness at the upper arms and shoulders, the weight taking hold there, packing in; he saw the slack, plump roll of the belly, the widening at the waist—that thickening which, it had been surveyed and studied in the business, the young people in the movie houses spotted and resented, perhaps wthout even knowing what they resented, which from their vantage point and youth they found repellent and wouldn't accept. What affected Claris particularly was a certain undercurrent running in her—a life and death anxiety to beat off the dread or desolation fast closing in on her. It was as though she was determined not to let this dread get the better of her or even to concede that it could touch her; as though she knew that if she gave in to it she would be finally swamped and pulled down forever. "If I forgot anything, he reminded me. I didn't believe he had such a thorough knowledge of my transgressions. He must have a special notebook where he writes it all down." She spoke in harsh, abrupt bursts, lingering now on the harangue by Case, when he had presented his list of indictments and had exposed her.

"Is this the best you can do, to stay shut up in the closeness and heat?" Claris said. "Does it make sense?"

"I wasn't sure I'd see you again. I thought we had lost you. I thought you have given up on me. I suppose that ruins my stock with you." She was back on the harangue again, on the sharp dressing-down by Case. "He didn't leave much to the imagination. That makes two of you. They like a woman who has something in reserve and can fight back on even terms. It's no good to them unless there's a certain amount of resistance to build up the excitement and make it interesting."

He didn't answer. She had it against him that he didn't speak, that he was one of the silent ones and kept controlled—if you had to go gingerly and be two-faced and watch what you said, you didn't talk. The door was still unlocked—he hadn't thought to turn the bolt over when he had come into the room—and for a moment he wondered what would happen, how it would seem, if someone by accident wandered in on them. She was ridden out with doubts and shame, the mortifications which she had gone away to England hoping to put behind her once for all and which Case—in his fervor, not meaning to batter her or cause her harm, as Claris had seen—had rammed home again and fully revived. Claris thought of the stories he had heard told about her —a fight in a taxicab, a notorious brawl in a Madrid hotel suite when a marriage had just begun, when it had foundered during the honeymoon—and he could see how these stories and the others, which she knew everyone must know, since they were, after all, part of the gossip around town, must weigh on her, how they must incapacitate her, making her shrink back and feel marked and conspicuous, making every meeting and occasion an agonizing ordeal for her. He could see why she everlastingly castigated herself for a mélange of missteps and gaffes, occurrences which, if he could only speak to her and explain, she would realize weren't gaffes at all, which, if they came from anyone else, would be negligible and be unnoticed, but which, coming from her, became blown up in her mind and distorted and a needless, continuing torment. But he couldn't speak to her; it was too late to start untangling the fears and apprehensions in which she was lost. She was devastated because she couldn't work. In the past, she had had the bustle at the studio, the day-to-day shooting schedules and demands on her, to keep her going, and so it was a double misfortune for her that she was bogged down and blocked, a paralysis that came about because she was distraught, because she didn't know what she could offer, because every idea she had withered and fell away from her. She had been out of action for the year and a half. She didn't know anything about acting, never had, would be the first to say so, and, in addition, she knew that what was required went beyond acting, that technical competence and training really had little to do with it. She was looking for those intangible values, hideously slippery and indefinable, coming out of nowhere, which made a job of work hit; which gave a roundness, an excitement, a constant promise of good things to come, a surprise; which made it possible for the performer to take to the stage. She wanted to find again those inner resources, some mystery of personality, which she had or thought she had when she was young and which she felt had been suddenly taken away from her. Nothing was good enough. She saw no reason why anything she might do on the stages should be spunky and alive and compel interest, and so she faltered in a steady anxiety and couldn't get to a start. She was overwhelmed by the magnitude of the financial ruin she had brought on Wigler, now that she had finally managed to kill off the production for him; and as Claris saw her glancing at him and then glancing away, not caring to take her troubles to him because she plainly had no trust in him and knew no great comfort was forthcoming from him, as he saw the panic churning in her to the point where she felt like someone plunging headlong from the top of an eighty-story skyscraper, the guilt and discontent went rankling through him. He looked to himself. He was still used up from the morning he had put in, from the grotesque events already indistinct and seeming unreal to him and which he grimly reminded himself he would make sure became even more shadowy and unreal as time went by, sideslipping and palming his disabilities in the stylish way he had learned all his lifetime so that he could maintain presence and go on. The image of the cold, unfriendly rented rooms he had lived in came back to him. He saw himself on the move, attaching himself to groups, always on the fringes. He faced the sloth, the waste and inertia, the shameful seepage of the will and lack of belief in himself that he had let take away his strength and send him scurrying after disreputable schemes and easy ways out.

He told her about the reporters, that they were on to him and had discovered he was the new man in her life. He talked to her about these things to fill up the silence, to help bring her out of herself, because the reporters would be catching up with them sooner or later, would come clamoring at them with their barrage of questions, and because he and Adele had this grimy little chore also to look forward to. Claris could see the reporters smacking their lips over the new-found tidbit—the super-markets, the prominent California family, his connection with them—and he knew the columnists would now be able to run a full extra day's enjoyment out of this vital complication. He didn't know when she had eaten last, and thought he ought to get some food in her. "We could go to a drive-in. We could manage it," he urged her. She wouldn't be seen or it would be only a carhop. They'd be in and out before anyone knew it. "You have to have something," he said. But she didn't hear him, just as she probably hadn't heard a word when he had talked to her about the movie reporters, and the ploy failed. He couldn't get her to start thinking of walking out of the room if that had been his intention and the real reason he wanted her to have something to eat.

"I have a headache," she said. "I don't feel well. I know. You told me. These things take care of themselves. The morning comes. You wake up and everything is fine. The moral is never to cut your throat." Claris had lolled about on the different movie lots, had absorbed the feeling of the life there, and in the slovenliness and despair, as he waited on her, the contrast caught in his mind—how it was for her now, how it had once been, in the beginning days, when she had first come on those golden walks and streets. The studio lots, with their acres of standing sets, Western streets, railroad depots, outbuildings and departments, were, each of them, brimming, enclosed worlds of their own, and he could see her taking her place in that privileged community, emboldened after her clean-scoring successes, knowing she belonged, ready to go with anything. Claris had been in an executive dining room, in a studio office, when one or another of the fortunate few came by—

smiling and vigorous, envied, knowing they were envied, with that amazing pearly radiance they had. "She'll do well. She'll make it. She works hard, is selfish and willing to lose weight." They believed they were apart from the ordinary run, keeping this assurance to themselves only for the sake of propriety, out of regard for the feelings of their friends and the people around them; they believed they were under a guiding star, as if that radiant beauty would hold its perfection and stay unmarred forever. And thinking of the new ones on the rise whom he had watched at their peak, before the awakening set in, before that secret condescension they felt for people suddenly turned around on them, confounding and throwing them in disarray as they saw they were in the end no different from the others whom they had hitherto so cavalierly dismissed, he captured vividly the picture of Adele for whom the rise must have been even more unsettling, considering how young she had been, the poor background she had come away from and the stunning speed with which she had gone to the top of the heap, and he could imagine what the recollection must do to her, how she must consume herself with longing as she looked back to those sun-filled days when it all went easily and it seemed nothing she put her hand to could miss.

She was on the brink, liable to go teetering off in some convulsive break at any moment. Claris was familiar with the vagaries of these disruptions; he had been through the state himself, in those besieged empty rented rooms, when you fumbled and reached, when you waited for the phone to ring, for something to happen, for a deliverance to come in from somewhere, and so he knew exactly what was going on with her. All her life whatever she had wanted she had wanted with a fierce intensity, and she was still the same person now that everything was against her. She wouldn't accept her condition, refused to accept it, fought it steadily and head on, and since there was no solution or palliation, no way of resolving the fright and unhappiness that festered in her, the result was a merciless, minute-by-minute, non-stop abrasion, too much to be borne and yet clinging on, never diminishing. "You made a bad selection," she said. "You never know what you're getting when you go in with a lady friend on a spree. That's one of the hazards. Look at him—how daintily he treats me, standing still there, afraid to say anything that might upset me and start me off." She chipped at him, taking him to task because he humored her, taking it out on him because she had been besmirched and had besmirched herself in the run-in with Case the evening before and he had been there to witness it. "You had yourself a front-row seat to the whole production," she said. Claris didn't respond, holding her down, retreating before her, so to speak, hoping that she would expend herself and eventually get the jitters out of her system by taking it out on him, and as he persevered with her, telling himself it was a disagreeable stretch, an interval of time to be lived through, that it had to be this way or else how could he move in on her and take her, a wave of exasperation, of helplessness, rose in him. He was looking on ahead to what still had to be done and what lay before him—the business of tipping her around, of getting her to go in with him on his plan, the falsity and deception that would ensue, she knowing and he knowing and both of them proceeding in the pretense of decency and good heart. He resented the need to feel sorry for her. He resented her for the woes she ceaselessly insisted on inflicting on herself. Anyone who went near her was drawn in and enslaved, forced to be concerned solely with her activities and derangements, and the worst of it, as Claris knew, was that the enslavement did her no good—the brunt of the grief remained with her. She went right on sopping up the punishment, and in the end, after all the trouble she gave, after making herself objectionable and a burden, she wound up with just another mortification to add to her collection and belabor herself with. She had once been married—early in the game, during the first flush of her success—to a man now widely known for his interest in the amenities, for the elegance of his home, for his standing in that busy social interchange which occupied certain segments of the community and on which they prided themselves. It was a pairing so unlikely that if Claris hadn't known they had actually been married, he would never have been able to believe it, and the very distance—between Adele and the life this former husband represented, at which she had failed—served to point up to her her shortcomings in a way that

must be a daily, living reproach to her, served to make
it clear why she felt as she did toward the stylish ladies
here at the hotel or wherever else she might see them,
those persons so well-mannered and secure, making love
with a necklace of beads on, with a ribbon around their
hair. "I could tell you stories about these pussycats that
would make your hair stand," she had said to Claris, but
even as she flailed at them, that time and the other times,
he knew how much she would have given if she could
only be part of them and had what they had. They
were at ease with any group, knew the right doctors,
flew in decorators from Texas and New York, and she
understood she was nowhere in the same class, she
who had never had a home for long and had passed from
husband to husband. She couldn't rest or resign herself.
She had to be always at top speed, always before the
firing squad. "Living out their lives in Sherman Oaks and
Chatsworth," she had said to Claris, speaking of some
actresses she knew; she had had to be on the fashionable side of the hills—Holmby Hills, Bel-Air, Beverly
Hills. It was out of this same restlessness and sheer
wanting that she had come to waste the last year
and a half traveling about from place to place in Europe.
The Hollywood infatuation with the international jet-set
high life really had to do with television, with the in-
roads the television sets made on the box-office receipts;
the movie crowd swung over to Rome and London for the
budgets, the cheaper production costs, the government
subsidies. But with the flair that characterized a good

139

many of these people, with their bustling spirits and showman's sense of pleasure, they had talked it up big, and, since whatever was around the bend held an allure, since what other people had always evoked a pang and envy, the continental scene soon took on a shine and became a wonder. And so, in order to get her own back, to recoup everything at a stroke and have a triumph over the ladies, she had gone into this marriage with the Englishman, putting her hopes on yachts and the favored mooring posts in the harbor. She made a specialty of torturing herself. Knowing the idiosyncrasies of her makeup as he did, that unlucky self-consciousness that afflicted her, he knew how she detested herself for her brawls and excesses even as she was engaged in them. He had watched her these last weeks, driving herself without stint, rushing willfully into catastrophe, fighting to the limits of her strength and then pushing herself on to find new strength so that she could fight some more. Even now when she was beaten and it was over, she wouldn't give up. Claris thought of this thing she had just done—breaking in on Louis, making the flight in the dark to bury herself, out of a desperate wish to be no longer seen or heard of, and also, since nothing with her could be uncluttered, causing this newest sensation in a last-ditch bid for attention, to keep them all coming at her and worrying about her, Case included. To the public the behavior of people like Hogue was incomprehensible, a show of temperament indulged in by the actresses because they were spoiled, foolhardy, overly im-

pressed with their importance. But Claris had been in the
room with her, in the electric light. He had seen her
sick, the stomach turning over in her, the body going
suddenly unstrung, that uncontrollable fluttering or
racing taking possession of her. He tried to drive these
meanderings and misgivings from his mind. She had no
choice, he told himself—as a matter of hard practicality,
she would have to go in with him, so in the end he would
have the working partnership he wanted. Whatever com-
punctions he might have he would get over, he told himself, just as in the past, when he had had to squirm
through some unholy mess or other, he had always managed to find it in him to comfort himself and survive.
Nor in the welter, as he stayed with her, silently counter-
ing and giving ground, according to his tactic, did he
miss the joke on himself, the incongruity, that he should
be bothering himself with remorse and fine shadings of
sensibility, he who had lived by small larcenies all his
life and was yet so constituted that this morning, when
he was busy trying to use his child to get a cash settlement out of his in-laws, he could be startled, genuinely
amazed that he was in fact doing this. She lay back in
the chair—lackluster, loose, indifferent. She had been re-
vealed to Claris. One by one the details of her life had
been brought out to the light before him, a stripping
away which she more than anyone must find grating,
but she brushed aside all restraint and let him stare—because they were in the room together and she had no
one else, because it was just another crudity along with

the rest of the crudities and defeats she could do nothing about and had to live with. She dispensed with the guise, that artificial personality we put out for the sake of appearances, to get us through a meeting, when for one reason or another the heart is out of us, so that it often happens that we are two or three persons, depending on the sets of people we are with and the throw of the circumstances that have brought us to these different groups. He saw her as she had always been—improvident, ill-equipped, precipitate. She had never had the quality of the women-guests at the hotel, those soft-spoken women who not only had little to say but seldom even listened, who, in their relationships with men, offered an ardor overwhelmingly tender and solicitous and at the same time impersonal, a kindness which they could discontinue seemingly without an instant's feeling or trace of remembrance.

She roused, pulling herself to her feet in an odd, abrupt surge of movement that puzzled Claris until he realized that she was gasping, that she was fighting to get her breath. The mass of nervous ailments which harrowed her never let her alone for long. If it wasn't the scalp-burning, the stitches in the side of her head, the angina, the overbreathing, then it was the eyes going out on her, refusing to focus and producing those gauzy, bluish spots, so that other people in turn became speckle-eyed and shifty before her. The neurotic manifestation this time took the form of suffocation. She simply didn't breathe, a failure due to an involuntary constriction of the throat or diaphragm, or else it was that she just forgot to take the trouble to breathe. The seizure crept up on her—suddenly, as she lay there, she felt herself sinking away; suddenly she was swallowing for air. "You have to get up and start walking around or else you'll strangle to death," she said. "You have to start learning how to breathe all over again." She ran on, going off now on some theory she had evidently figured out for herself, one of the superstitious fancies with which she encumbered herself as if she hadn't enough to muddle herself with. She was blocked, she said; there was nothing she could do to help herself. God or something of the kind was hammering down on her, meting out a prearranged, astrological ordering of events which neither she nor anyone else could alter. She believed that payment had to be made, that she was now paying for the good things, the dazzling successes, that had been given to her, that it always worked out in this way, according to a sinister, unknowable pact. She claimed that everyone who had risen to the top and was in the public eye was blighted somewhere in the background in this manner, that they all carried with them a secret sorrow, a taint which affected them or a child or whoever was close to them.

He broke out at her. It got to him—the two of them perspiring in the heat, huddled in the room over the kitchen. "Why do you talk such nonsense?" He couldn't make things right for her. He couldn't bring back the years. He was tired of struggling with her neurotic

143

afflictions, her hallucinations, the endless string of her
troubles, miseries which were real and incontrovertible
and which he wished he didn't have to know, which he
had really tried to run away from when he had driven off
the place in his rush the night before. He lashed out at
her—she had just blown a fortune of money. She was in
debt. She hadn't stopped until she had smashed the picture and brought everything down on her. She had the
whole town against her. She was alone, she who couldn't
fend for herself when the going was good, who always
had to have someone to cry to and hold her up. "Who
have you got to go to? Who can help you? Can you
carry it by yourself? Don't you see what you're forcing
me to do?" Whether he wanted to take her or didn't
want to take her had nothing to do with it. It wasn't up
to him. He had to move in on her. There was no one
else. They would go hand in hand now, doting on each
other, loving. He would be in business, one of the smooth
operators, prospering and living off her, and as he bore
down on her in this wild, irrational charge, blaming her
for the injury he was doing to her, he heard the whine
in his ears, the ever-present mediocrity which he had
never been able to beat.

She came apart, every guard down, every license per-
mitted. Who was he to hold forth over her? What did he
think she was going to do, stand there and listen to his
strictures? If he thought he knew so much about her,
then she wanted him to know the rest—the reasons why
she had come to be as she was, the offenses committed

against her, worse, the offenses she herself had committed, not meaning to do them, meaning to do them,
acting out of fear, out of greediness, out of ignorance,
because she had been new and raw and hadn't known
what was expected of her or how she was supposed to
behave. What poured out was the black devastation,
when you sit in a room and silently hope to draw strength
and an anchoring just from being with people; what
poured out was that feeling of dissolution, impossible to
express or make clear to another, normally held tight
and secret, but which she was now determined to get out
of her and share. She told him of one remembered
abomination, of a drive home from the racetrack with
one of her husbands—the mismatch, the husband who
was too old for her, when they all said she was looking
for a father figure. They had invited a young couple
to spend the afternoon with them, so they had their
guests as spectators in the car when the squabble broke
out, the afternoon having gone badly, the whole idea of
the outing having misfired and fizzled. She didn't spare
Claris or herself. She gave the occurrence in all its
ugliness—the ferocity, the language, "I'll get you in the
crotch," the old man rearing back on the seat, holding
his crotch for protection, the young couple taking in the
scene, the chauffeur's eyes busy in the rear-view mirror,
too. "Does the taste surprise you? Is it on the question-
able side? Do you think the lummox doesn't know she's
a lummox?" She ground the words out to him. "All
right," she said, "so we've heard the stories. We know all

about the little fool, the fights and marriages one after the other." She wanted him to know how it was from the participant's point of view, away from the dinner parties and the gossip. She wanted him to know how it was when they woke up the next morning, after the fact, after the calamity and horror, whatever the outrage had been, when they saw the face that appeared before them in the bathroom mirror—the times when they didn't make a break for it and run away and hide themselves from sight. "Yes, I know more now. If I had it to do all over again I'd be better prepared. I had to have it on the table, everything out in the open. I'd come off sweeter the second time around, but what good is it? How does it help me?" She dredged up from the past the mean, hateful memorabilia which she alone knew, which everyone else had forgotten, telling of an incident on the set when she had been standing by between shooting takes, when a troop of visitors had been brought along; in a fit of giddiness, for reasons she didn't understand and would never understand, because she thought it was the smart thing to do, because the pressure was on her, she had brandished her breasts at the sightseers and called out, "Brew One-O-Two, Pabst Blue Ribbon." She told him of an abominable moment with her mother, this in the soaring early days when it was all starting to hit and come together for her, when she had already been at the door, on her way out with a man on a date or something along those lines, and, in her incredible, blundering stupidity, had had to turn back—"Why don't you too,

Momma?" she had said to her mother. "Why not? It's good for you, healthy. I'll fix it up. I'll get you a friend." She told Claris of an abortion she had had to manage by herself, when she had first entered the lists, when she had been gulled, led on, used, run out on. "If I saw him again, I wouldn't spit in his eye," she said, but the vituperation wasn't meant for this far-distant partner— it was meant for herself, that she had been so abject, so impoverished and unequipped. She spoke of the seedy business district in the daylight, the vacant room over the store in Santa Monica, the doctor saying to her, "If you scream I'll throw you right out into the street." She jumped the years. She was talking about her mother, the way she had died, the emergency call and the things that had happened then. Her mother had been living in the Bay Area, in one of the cities outside of San Francisco, and Adele had had to pull herself together in the haste, forgetting the studio alarms and involvements, going up there alone, as it fell out, without a companion or friend. She had taken a room at the hotel nearest to the hospital, so that she would be close at hand, so that she could settle in for the siege, the business of hospital visiting, of going to and fro, and as she sped on, rigorously giving the full, lacerating account, he saw that what she was really trying to do with him was reach out for a dispensation and release. She told how it had all recoiled on her—the way she had lived, the bickering and struggling to maintain status, the fretting, the going to the topline directors of the moment, begging them,

"Tell me what to do. Tell me what to do." It had all fallen away from her, and, since Claris had been in these straits himself, he understood from his own experience how she had felt and what she was trying to explain to him. It was a time for summing up, for self-recriminations—the omissions crowding in, the instances of neglect, of ingratitude, the persons cold-shouldered and failed, the pitiless, incessant, well-founded demands made on her when she herself was beyond her strength and it was all she could do to keep her head above water. She told of the stealth, the unreality she had moved in, people starting to stare at her, spotting her, muttering to themselves, "Who was that? Wasn't that . . . ?" She hadn't had the courage or presence of mind to go out for her meals—it had been a fourth-rate hotel, one of the older, leftover structures, without dining-room facilities; she hadn't had the wit to send someone out for the food she needed, and so had found herself in the blaze of the all-night supermarket, haunting the shelves, looking for tomato juice, for tuna fish. She spoke of the hours at the bedside, her mother there inhuman and far away in the great, inconceivable, searing pain, and the woman neighbor, her mother's friend, sitting alongside, mourning and moaning softly, "Why didn't you help her, Adele?" "It was cancer," she cried out to Claris. "What could I have done? You can't fight cancer. I couldn't have saved her life and made her well again. Why was the blame on me?" But it was true, what the neighbor woman had said was true, and Adele knew it. She had

flung out of the hospital, she told Claris, not even going
back to the hotel, leaving them there with something
more to wonder about, mystifying them completely, and
the memory of this final default remained to burn in her
too. "I used to believe people committed suicide because
they were sick or hopeless or trying to make someone
feel sorry for them. It's not that," she said. "You lose connection. Something happens to you. People who are close
to you, whom you've known for years, suddenly become
strangers and you don't know who they are or what
they have to do with you. You don't feel anything. You
can't love anything or anyone. You can't work. That's
why they kill themselves."

He left her alone. The barriers were down. Everything was said, so they had reached that wry understanding from which they could now go on, and he knew
she would soon be ready to leave with him, that he would
have her out of the room. In the distress between them,
he considered all that had gone before with her, the scale
of her doings, the force and commotion. It came back
to him how she had had it in her from the beginning—
in those easy high school days, when the seven or eight
motion picture companies dominated the life of the city—
to take on the big risks, to strike out boldly for the top
scores, looking even then for the enhancement and importance she knew she had to have. He only had to think
of her conglomeration of neurotic symptoms to realize
the fanatic energy she had put in, the energy which was
more than people were willing to exert or could exert and

which was what, after all, made the difference. He saw her in the concourse at the high school, the skirt hitched up at the waist, because it didn't fit, because it was her mother's; he saw her in the first enterprising venturings—caught in lies, waiting for the maid to leave, the blush, the wickedness and temptation. Fannie had pleaded with her, others had taken a hand—at the agency, at the studio—but there had been nothing anyone could do to keep her from the succession of husbands. She had been up against the good-looking boys, those idlers and ne'er-do-wells who, for all their idleness, worked industriously on their manner, everything calculated to provide that limber amiability which caused people to want to be with them. They could be wonderfully persuasive in private, with their playmaker's sincerity, that actor's game of illusion that went on among them apart from the acting on the stages. They had about them an airiness, a promise of vivacity and pleasure, as fraudulent and short-lived as it was enticing; and even though she had just been through one disaster of a marriage and had learned her lesson, even though she had been through the aftermaths, the vindictiveness, the eviction notices and lawsuits, she would plunge straight into the next mess, aware of what she was doing and of the probable consequences but actively following out her misfortune, contrary and perverse, as if believing she had a right to her folly. She had gone repeatedly back to Case, caught up in this erratic relationship which had tortured itself out over the years and was also part of the commotion of her life. She had gone after Case—Claris had seen how she hadn't rested until she had contrived to bring him out to the hotel-resort. She had made the overtures, had been the one to weep and carry on in those steamy eruptions behind locked doors; and Case, for reasons of his own, in the obstinate way of these arrangements, had chosen to keep on with her, however his attachment appeared to outsiders and whatever he let them make of it. She had stayed close to him in a wary, hostile proximity, accepting the abuse and grudges that accrued with the years, knowing he had the full record on her, which was what she meant when she said he made her feel like nothing—she had stayed close to him because she at least knew what she had in him, because she had had to have his devotion and need. She had had no allegiance to him or affection, had felt free to go to other men, to marry, and yet if he wasn't there to spy on her she would become instantly stricken and contrite and would go into a decline. Because she had this problem with her clothes, everything at the moment either too big for her or too small, she had resorted—in the weeks Claris had been with her—mainly to wrap-around dresses; and in his mind's eye, in thinking about her and how it must have been for her in the years past, even though she was in the room before him now, he had the vision of her in one of the wrap-around dresses, agitated and provoked, moving in stride, as he had seen her so often, the lace yoke of her slip showing, the breasts there bobbing and heaving. Without the razzle-dazzle, the achievement and attention, she would be nothing, somebody on a parking lot, a passer-by in the street, and he saw her constantly embattled, fighting off the whittlers and belittlers and whoever would bring her down, fighting off the dinginess of heart, the ogre, which she had abhorred from the outset and had been determined to best. She had known she wasn't the strongest person, or if she hadn't known, then Case and Fannie had made it sufficiently clear when they argued with her that she exhausted herself and had no stamina, but she had driven herself on with her flamboyant, unsparing tenacity, and Claris wondered now at her illnesses, at the mauling she had absorbed in her time —the curettages, the operations, the bad operation, the babies before that, the brutal intensive reducing regimens, when, to meet a shooting schedule and get herself in shape, she installed herself in the hospital and they systematically sloughed the weight off her, so that she herself came to view her body with a sick distaste. It was all of a piece, the patches and pictures all coming together—musing on her in this way, he could still see her bustling down the high school paths, rapt in the glow of that time, in the butterfly kisses, the women's magazines, the competition and the thrill of expectation, all things then being possible and seeming just around the turn for the having, and it occurred to him, if these impressions were so bright and immediate in his mind, how much more recent they must be to her, and he could understand the fury in her, the rage of disbelief and bewilderment, now that all this which she had fought for so desperately was so soon being taken away from her. He understood the loathsome brevity of time, the rapidity with which it goes—the flabbiness of thighs, the changes coming on one after the other, the face transforming itself into somebody else's, the catch at the heart when you suddenly one day realize how old you are. She had told him a story about herself, this in one of the countless confessions and effusions when they had been together and the time had gone by—a story of an encounter with a salesman in a used-car lot in the auto row at Culver City. She had told the story on herself, going back to the days when she was unknown and hardpressed, as so many of them liked to do, the contrast appealing to them, no doubt, because it gave them an inner confidence, a continuing renewal of courage. She had managed to be invited that afternoon to a gathering at one of the glittering west Los Angeles homes, and she had wanted this certain car on display, whether she could make the full down payment on it or not, because she was young, because she had the image of herself arriving at the party on her own. The feeling of the Culver City area of the period came to Claris—the empty lots, the wide boulevards with sandy, neglected islands in the middle of them, the sun pouring down, so still and breathtakingly brilliant, as it was in those earlier years. Claris had been to a number of the lavish afternoon house parties. He had seen the young girls who were brought out to help dress up the gatherings. He had watched them arrayed on the grounds, on the mats and chaises around the swimming pools, making themselves at home, with their marvelous adaptability, as though they had lived in these rich, beautiful surroundings all their lives and had never known anything else, so he could tell, from the behavior and quiet resolution on the faces of the girls he had observed, what the occasion must have meant to Adele and how deeply she must have wanted to be there. She had finished with the salesman, she had known what to do. She had gotten through the pawing, the clutching and embraces, and had gone speeding off, putting the distance behind her, as though the incident had never happened and there had never been such a man.

THEY WERE TRUNDLING up
the walk to the main building, Fannie and Case, and as
she marched with her ex-husband at her side, she thought
of the stucco mansion they had lived in when they had
come out to California, the showplace home up on the
hill on LaBrea Avenue in Hollywood, with the private
driveway, the electric gate and the talk-box; guests had
to be careful what they said when they drove up and
waited for the gate to open—every word could be heard
up at the house. The reporters had had it right for once.
There was truth to the stories, the thing going on right
under their noses. Adele was off on another fling. Fannie
and Case had known ever since the disappearance that
Claris was the man involved—the people from the talent
agency had told them so—but they hadn't known about
the steward's room over the kitchen, that she had been
hiding out there, and it was the letdown now, the alarm
over, the anxieties quelled, the two of them allowed to
breathe again for a while until the next crisis broke

out. "Keep him away from me," Case said. "If I see him, I'll hit him in the belly. I'll give him an uppercut." Claris had brought her back to the bungalow. Fannie had been in to see them, was having a tray sent over, and Case had picked her up on her way back to the office in the hotel lobby—she still had the morning's work to clear up, the invoices, the checks. Case blustered and rumbled but was only going through the motions. There wasn't the sting, the rush of blood, it wasn't the same as the other times when Adele had started a new romance and he had gone crazy, and Fannie knew it. He was interested in wrapping it up, in getting back to Las Vegas. He talked about Adele, still concerned, wondering how it would be with her now, if the new man could do anything for her. She wasn't getting any younger, he told Fannie.

"What do you think, you got older and she got younger? It don't go like that. What did you expect?" The trouble was, to him, in his eyes, she had never changed—she was always the Wampas Baby Star. Fannie had noticed the look on Case's face last night when he had finally seen Adele without the rose-colored glasses, as she was, a woman getting on, the same as everyone else, and it had been a pang; Fannie didn't know why and it still annoyed her. She had been the homely one, left out and taken for granted, in another department, and still she had genuinely felt for him and for Adele too, because the great passion, which was theirs, not hers, had worn itself out and was gone.

"Who is he?" Case said.

"A man. What the hell. Another husband, another marriage—marriage two hundred and twelve." She had been in the bungalow and had talked to them, but that didn't mean she knew any more than Case did and she couldn't help him out. She walked away from him in the lobby, going on straight to the office, leaving him to pack and start preparing for the trip to Las Vegas. Her heels went rapping over the tiles. She walked away without a backward glance, pushing out the memories, trying to think of the work she had waiting for her, telling herself that if she had it to do all over again, knowing what she knew now, would she be any the wiser; would it be any different; would she be able to steer it along a different course; would she be able to influence him in the least and tell him what to do? She had known better than anyone else what it had meant to him; even in those days when she was the one getting hurt and knew she figured to lose in the long run, even while it was happening, she had imagined it as he imagined it, as it all took hold in him—the cars, the luxury, the homes, the Santa Anas blowing in through the canyons and passes, the women they had here, the movie stars. She had known what he had done in order to make it out to the coast—when he was mixed up with the slot machines, the cherries, apricots, and pears, when he was trying to get in and the parties in control rejected him and wouldn't even let him talk to them. She had lived through the showdown fight with the muscle men, that time when she had been in fear and trembling for his life. "Look out below!" he had yelled the eight times from the roofs. They had broken up eight of his machines for a sign, and he hadn't been able to eat, he hadn't been able to sleep, the fire burning in him. She had warned him they would maim him, but there had been no way of tying him down and holding him in the house. He had gone to eight of their candystore locations, had carried the heavy slot machines up to the roof one after the other, smashed them down on the pavement three and five stories below, and then they had been finally willing to see him. They had called him in. "I wanted to give but nobody would take," he had said to them and the remark had amused them. They had looked him over a second time and decided they could use him. And the doors had opened wide.

She had gone along with the show, not knowing what they needed it for or what she was doing, but doing it, every morning getting up and starting out again, making herself over and adjusting herself to fit in with the high-class company and not shame anyone, and it had come hard for her—she would start out in those days for I. Magnin's or Harry Cooper's to spend the money and find herself at Ohrbach's. She had been at the hairdresser's at Saks, talking to Mr. Don and Mr. George and the lady receptionist at the desk, ingratiating herself so that she would be known and greeted by name and be also in the swim, when she had heard the news, learning about Adele and the full-blown affair in the beauty salon, which was where they always heard it, over the partitions, except that at Saks they hadn't had partitions, and it had been a blow.

"Fannie, it's true. I love her and she loves me," he had announced to her, very formal and civilized, when she had presented him with the story, and it had bitten deep, the anger going through her, not for herself and all she had endured with him, but for him—that he could have deluded himself to such an extent, living big, taking himself seriously. "You love her and she loves you— over my dead body," Fannie had told him, getting herself together, going to work. "You fool," she had said to him, "don't you know to them you're a freak? Don't you know they go with you because they think you're a gangster and it gives them a kick?" "Fannie, I'm sorry. That's the way it is and that's the way it's going to be," he had said to her, and then had gone back to Adele to find out that at the last minute she wanted to beg off, that she was busy at the time with the other fellow, with another fiancé. "Here," Fannie had said to him, seeing him pine and what the disappointment was doing to him, "you wanted the goddam divorce, take it." But she had seen to it that she didn't suffer in the meantime; she had gotten everything that was coming to her.

There had been the hot, rambunctious flurries of the first years, when he had tracked Adele on the desert rambles, when he had put friends on her, gotten reports on the phone. It had shaken down into this hard and fast pattern, the two of them unable to let go of each other over the interruptions, the marriages, and absences. He had had her in mind, one of those men tough in business or whatever they spent their time on, with the chopped-up faces, with their down to earth big-league savvy and smart catch-phrases, a corner reserved in them, a soft spot. They hung on and took the knocks, because they liked it that way, because it gave them something to think about and filled out their lives. He had been on the sidelines when she had gone ahead with the Canadian fellow, the man who had retired and come down to California to live and who had been a good twenty-five years older than she was. The wedding had been the gala of the year—the whole hotel ballroom redecorated, a hundred and twenty-five dollars a place setting, the table napery and the gowns of the bridesmaids matching. There had been a kind of reception line, the new husband proudly introducing Adele to the guests at the wedding, and they had stood there like two wooden statues facing each other: "How do you do, Mrs. Whatever the name was," he had said to her, and she had said to him, "How do you do, Mr. Case."

He had been around at the beginnings, and then at the deadfalls. When she had hurried away from the hospital that time, somebody had had to go back to attend to the arrangements—the death certificate, the funeral, the closing up of the place her mother had lived in—and so, for this reason and all the other reasons, she had found herself with him again in that series of departures and returnings. He had still had the house on LaBrea Avenue, the second-hand paradise, and they had been together on the grounds, he on one side of the pool, she on the other side, walking by herself in the dark glasses, a figure in a dress, something still there, the body still having it for him—the shiver, the attraction. The nerve had been fading fast; she had had the feeling—the downhill drift, the scare, the need for prayers. For the others who had traveled over to Europe, because that was where the pictures were being made, it had been the old partying again, but she hadn't belonged in that clique, just as she had never been one of them when they were all back in Hollywood. She had understood what she was doing when she had taken on the titled Englishman. There had been the acclaim and respect tendered to her, the deference that went with being a movie star, and in this world of celebrity, of fast movement and shiny living, she had thought there might very well be a place for her too, that it could just possibly be a way. She hadn't expected wonders. She had set out this time to be sensible, to make the best of it, as people did. She had held on to the last, putting up with her husband and his friends, with their savage, hard-running play, using up the money she had had, doing everything in her power to stay with the marriage and keep from coming home where she hadn't anyone or anything she wanted to come back to.

THE WOMEN-GUESTS were grouped at the tables on the terrace, providing a background for the press conference Adele was holding to announce her engagement. "Again the catering to them, again the fixing their coffee, putting in the sugar and cream, stirring it for them," a woman at one of the tables said, referring—it wasn't clear—either to the new liaison coming into being, or to the married couple who had had the open altercation and had reconciled, who were also there, or to herself. They had all been in the business at one time or another, as stand-ins or stock girls, understood the exigencies, had made their own adjustments, and they looked on in the evening quiet, happy to lend a hand, not approving and not disapproving. The two little boys, the twins, were running wild, tripping over the television cables, bumping into the news cameramen, having themselves a time. Fannie was going after them, struggling to hold onto them, one kid tearing free as she grabbed out for the other, and Case hurried over to help, boxing them in. "The little rats know they can get away with murder, so they take advantage," Fannie said, breathing hard. Somebody had given the twins Good Humors on a stick and now Case complained, "Why did they do that? Didn't they know it would make a mess and look lousy?" He and Fannie both were anxious for the press meeting to go off well. It was the best thing that could have happened under the circumstances. If the reporters wanted to blow up the romance, then it would be a ready-made cover, accounting for the turmoil of the last weeks, throwing a new light on the whole affair from the publicity standpoint. Adele had the debts, the lawsuits and back taxes, and needed the pictures as fast as she could get them. That was why she had had to go through with the announcement whether she was in the mood for it or not, and that was why Fannie and Case were fussing on the floor of the terrace with the twins, restraining them and keeping up appearances. Adele herself was over to the side, surrounded by a cluster of reporters. She handled the gaff, cool and in control, letting the press see for themselves that she was up to the mark, that she still looked good and could go on. Did she miss Europe, did she like it in Palm Springs, was she enjoying her visit? "Yes, so far so good," she said, not knowing what to answer, giving them anything for an answer. "Do you think this marriage will last?" "What?" "I mean, considering the track record—" She cut him off. She knew what he meant. "You'll be the first to know. When we come to the parting of the ways, we won't do a thing without getting in touch with you. Just leave us your name and the name of your newspaper and you'll have the exclusive," she said.

Claris came walking off the grounds toward the steps of the terrace, bringing Melanie with him. At the other end of the terrace, where it merged with the lobby of the hotel, Case and Fannie were still busy with the twins, delivering them to some of the Mexican chambermaids there for safekeeping. The reporters, seeing Claris approach, stepped back, clearing a path so that he and Melanie could get up to Adele and join her. The reporters followed Claris with their eyes, frankly admiring—because by sweet talk, by the luck of his physique, and by who knew what special wiles he had, he had won this still highly valuable partnership with Hogue and had pulled it off. Claris had gone back for Melanie. She had remained in the bungalow and had been almost overlooked. He knew how she felt and what she thought of him, and by going back for her, by showing he remembered her and wanted her to be with them, he had meant to attest to her that her fears would be proven groundless. He wanted to reassure her. He wanted to make it up to her, for her homeliness, for the terrible thick glasses and the pain that lay in wait for her, and as he went with her through the aisle of reporters, disregarding their stares, he vowed in his heart that whatever one person could do for another he would do for her.

Adele smiled as he came up, and made room for him beside her. They stood together, arm in arm. Transcending the ignominies that had passed between them, falling into the guise they would now assiduously practice with each other, they presented themselves to the onlookers, brazening it out, challenging them and uncaring. The press photographers darted about, getting their still pictures from all the different angles they seemed to require. The television people threaded in and out, tending to their equipment. In the activity going on around her, suddenly confused and oppressed by the activity, she turned her face up to Claris, forgetting her resolution, forgetting the crush or even where she was. She knew from her experience on the stages that anything she said would be picked up on the sound tracks, and whether it was for this reason or because of some other mental quirk, she formed the words to him, not speaking them or even whispering, just the lips moving soundlessly: I love you, I love you, I love you. The women sat at the tables. The reporters, the technicians surged about, all this in a time already gone by, the events recounted here having taken place some twelve years ago, when television was comparatively new and the big picture studios still throbbed, the collapse yet to come, the people enmeshed in their concerns, those pursuits, dreams, and diversions which occupy us so that we are each of us precious to ourselves and wouldn't exchange ourselves, the being in us, with any other, those wonderful moments which as they happen go by almost unnoticed but which return again and again in our thoughts to bemuse and warm us, the stir of smoking mountain panoramas, the ache of sweet summer days, of trees in leaf, of being in love, this prize, this treasure, this phantom life.

A Note on the Type

The text of this book is set in Monticello, a Linotype revival of the original Binny & Ronaldson Roman No. 1, cut by Archibald Binny and cast in 1796 by that Philadelphia type foundry. The face was named Monticello in honor of its use in the monumental fifty-volume *Papers of Thomas Jefferson*, published by Princeton University Press. Monticello is a transitional type design, embodying certain features of Bulmer and Baskerville, but it is a distinguished face in its own right.

The book was composed, printed, and bound by The Haddon Craftsmen, Inc., Scranton, Pennsylvania. Typography and binding design by Constance T. Doyle.